DEAD
SILENT

A gripping detective thriller full of suspense

HELEN H. DURRANT

Published 2016 by Joffe Books, London.

www.joffebooks.com

© Helen Durrant

ISBN-13: 978-1-911021-24-7

Prologue

In the thick fog of an early morning, a small white van could just be seen, weaving through the pouring rain along a distant country road.

"You've let me down, Vida. We were doing just fine, but that wasn't good enough for you. Was it?"

The man driving slammed his fist down on the dashboard. There were hot tears running down his face. He brushed a rough hand over his cheek. He could hardly see a thing — what with the tears, the rain pelting down hard and the fog, he was really up against it. Why did the weather have to be so foul when he had so much to do?

"You knew I loved you. I never gave you any reason to doubt it. We didn't need anyone else; we agreed. So why did you do it? You could have had anything — anything at all, but that!" He was screaming now, his eyes darting to the reflection in the rear-view mirror. There was no reply from the shape lying in the back.

"We talked. You said you felt the same as I did. But you didn't, did you? You still went and got yourself pregnant. Lying bitch! All along you had no intention of keeping our little bargain. I can't do it, Vida!" Screaming, shaking his head, as the anger built again. "You can't blame anyone else for what's happened — it's all your own stupid fault!"

The fog was so thick that the white van was now crawling along the narrow ribbon of a road, one of the country lanes above Hopecross. He'd have been better off on the bypass.

"You can't control yourself, that's your trouble. That's been the trouble with all of you stupid slags. Ten weeks, Vida, that's all we had, before you ruined everything," he sobbed. "After all I said. I poured my heart out, you selfish bitch. Stupid selfish bitch! You deserve what you've got coming — and more besides — for putting me through this!"

Almost blind with tears and rage, he swung onto the slip road that led down to the dual carriageway. It was devoid of traffic. On a normal day it would have been busy, even at this early hour of the morning. But today, in the fog, it was quiet. No need to crawl then, he decided, putting his foot down.

The van sped along towards Leesdon. He wasn't sure where he was going, where he was going to drop Vida off. He rubbed his forehead. He hadn't thought this through. The others had been easier — he'd simply kept them. But he didn't want to keep this one. Things were changing, and for the worse, so he'd get rid of her. But then all the others would have to go too. He was beginning to calm down. He had to think. It wouldn't be so bad; it'd be good to be rid of her. He wouldn't have to look at her whining face or scrawny body ever again.

Suddenly he saw a shape looming up in front of him. A dark mass was blocking the road and the occasional flame licked across the blackened sky. What the fuck was this? A car crash? Some sort of pile-up due to the weather? He strained his eyes to see, but in the fog he could make out nothing.

He skidded to an abrupt halt behind a large saloon car. The lights were out, and the bonnet had sprung up and was all twisted and bent. Spirals of steam rose from the engine. A man was screaming in pain in the front seat.

"I'm trapped!" he yelled out, seeing the headlights behind him. "I can't move my legs. Ring for help, please, for God's sake — do something!"

The van driver stood and looked at the scene in front of him. Multiple vehicles had ploughed into each other. Apart from the one man, an eerie silence, almost as thick as the fog itself, permeated the scene. No one moved. No one was coming. This was an opportunity he couldn't afford to miss.

"Out you get, bitch." He pulled a woman's body from the back of the van. He heard her feet thud hard on the tarmac, and he dragged her over to the saloon car. "This is the last time you cross me. I'll teach you to want what you can't have."

He yanked open one of the rear passenger doors and bundled her inside. She didn't make it easy for him; right to the end she was a pain in the backside. She was so heavy. A dead weight.

"Good riddance."

He riffled through the back of his van for a few minutes and returned with a petrol can. He casually emptied the contents under the saloon car, to increasing shrieks and screams for help from the trapped man. Surely he'd got it by now. There was no help coming.

Enough of this noise. He had things to do, places to go. He struck a match, casually flicked it under the car and walked away. Within a split second the vehicle was ablaze.

Like all the rest, Vida was now history.

Chapter 1

Day One

The weather had done its worst. Two late autumnal storms had brought down the last of the leaves, and underfoot the entire churchyard was a wet, slippery mess. At least the fog had mostly cleared. Some low swirling mist remained, clinging to the bleak hilltops.

Detective Inspector Tom Calladine stood silent, his daughter at his side, as the undertakers took his mother's coffin from the hearse. He must pull himself together. He had to get through this somehow. It had arrived; the day he'd pushed to the back of his mind, the event he hadn't wanted to think about. But now he had no choice. He wasn't sure he'd be able to get through it, but he had to hold it together for Zoe. She'd no sooner found her grandmother than she'd lost her again. This dying business was so final.

Zoe Calladine took hold of his hand and tugged it gently. "We should be going in," she whispered. "They're waiting for your signal."

He was dragging his heels, delaying things. He didn't want to admit that his mother was finally gone. She had slipped away in the dead of night without so much as a whimper. Why hadn't she fought? She wasn't really that old, not by today's standards. Surely there'd been a good few years still left in her?

He looked down at the young woman by his side. His daughter. Two months ago he hadn't been aware that she even existed. She'd come into his life like a bolt from the blue and was already leaving her mark. She planned to stay too, a decision she'd made with no prompting from him, and he was chuffed to bits about it.

She was still living with him but no doubt that'd change in time. Zoe was a solicitor, so she'd be able to afford a place of her own soon enough. She had studied law, got her degree and gained experience with a firm in Bristol. Now a local practice had taken her on.

Her help in organising all this had been invaluable. She'd dealt with the undertakers, as well as the wake at the Leesworth Hotel afterwards. In fact she'd done it all. As usual — stupid bugger that he was — he'd used the pressure of work as an excuse for failing to contribute.

She had made sure that all Freda's old friends knew. They were all here, too, and transport had been arranged for them. Monika had come, representing the care home his mother had lived in for the past few months. Monika looked drawn and nervous, every bit as upset as he was. She was shuffling about from one foot to another, and kept glancing at him. He caught her eye, but she merely nodded a curt greeting. He should have done things differently. She should have been standing with him. After all she was more than just his mother's carer, much more. God, he'd messed up there. Despite everything, he missed her.

But Lydia Holden had been the final straw that broke their relationship. It was true that it had been floundering for a while — not enough input from him — but after Lydia, Monika could barely bring herself to speak to him. He'd been trying to work out how to tell her about the beautiful reporter, but in the end he didn't have to. Monika had simply read Lydia's piece in the paper. She'd asked a few salient questions and no doubt quizzed Ruth, his sergeant, and worked out the rest for herself. Tom Calladine didn't love her, simple as that. How could he if his head could be turned so easily?

He looked towards the black-suited men who were arranging the flowers over the coffin. White lilies: traditional. His mother would have approved. He'd stood here before, almost on this same spot in fact, when he was twelve or thirteen, after his father died. He didn't remember feeling anything, really. He recalled hating having to wear a new suit, and that he'd been itching to get home to watch some telly programme or other — daft kid that he'd been back then.

His reverie was broken as a car on the drive caught his attention. A latecomer? He was about to go and meet whoever it was, but then swore under his breath. The car smoothing its way towards them was a sleek, black Bentley. That could mean only one thing.

Ray Fallon.

How the hell had he found out? More to the point, what did he think he was doing here? He hadn't bothered to visit when she'd been in the care home, so why attend her funeral? Apart from that, Ray Fallon knew damn well he wouldn't be wanted here.

"Thomas!"

Fallon was immaculate in what looked like an Italian designer suit, and a cashmere overcoat with a velvet collar. Last time they'd met, Fallon had been lying in a hospital bed following a major heart attack. Look at him now. The Devil surely did look after his own.

Calladine stepped forward to meet his cousin. What was the use? He supposed his mother would have wanted him here. She'd practically raised him, after all.

"Well, Thomas. Sad day." Fallon held out a hand, which Calladine ignored.

One of his goons leaned into the boot and handed across to the undertakers a huge arrangement of white roses that spelled out *Auntie Freda*. Over the top and totally unnecessary.

"They're all waiting. We'd better do this, Thomas." Fallon gestured his men forward. Three more black-suited goons got out of the car and made for the coffin. "You and I will take the front — you on the right, me on the left. Sort of apt, don't you think?"

Calladine didn't laugh. Ray Fallon was one of Manchester's most infamous villains. The only reason he wasn't doing life was because the team at Manchester Central weren't smart enough to nail him. Was he being too harsh on his colleagues? Fallon wasn't only clever, he was ruthless. He was a past master at ensuring watertight alibis, even if it meant committing murder to keep them that way. So it wasn't just about catching him. Trapping him and getting people to testify in court — that was the key. But in the meantime he continued to thrive. Not even a heart attack and bypass surgery had stopped him. The man was a menace, a pain in the arse — and, much to the inspector's embarrassment, his damned cousin!

The six men took hold of Freda Calladine's coffin and bore it into Leesworth Parish Church. If Mum was watching this, she'd be thrilled. But from Calladine's point of view it was the stuff of nightmares. His mother was being taken on her final outing, accompanied by Manchester's most dangerous gangster and his minions.

All the same, Calladine couldn't hold back a small chuckle. There was a weird irony in all this. He was just thankful that there was no one from the nick here to witness his embarrassment.

At the church door, Calladine took a deep breath. This was it. This was the final goodbye.

* * *

Everywhere was mad busy. It was only a few weeks until Christmas, and Leesworth appeared to be in panic mode. The shops along Leesdon High Street were enjoying a brief respite from the woes of the recession, and the garden centre was doing a roaring trade in all kinds of festive fare.

It was lunchtime and Cassie Rigby was playing up. She was hungry, and bored with being dragged around the shops. She was only four years old.

"You sit there and be a good girl." Anna was looking warily at the long queue at the self-service counter. "I will get you something — one of those kid's boxes. Is that okay?"

The little girl nodded. She liked them; they included a yoghurt plus a carton of juice.

Anna Bajek looked at the queue again. If she took Cassie with her they'd lose the table. "Look — you must stay here. You mustn't move. If you're good, then you can have ice cream afterwards, when we've seen Santa."

The child nodded and leaned back on the padded seat. Anna piled their shopping beside her and went to join the queue. She looked back and waved. The child would be okay; they were only a few feet apart.

The woman in front of Anna was arguing with the young man serving food behind the counter, hands on her broad hips. Why was there only ever one person on the job in these places?

"I ordered cottage pie. He wanted the soup with a roll."

The waiter disappeared into the back, while the queue of people waiting began rolling their eyes and complaining. After what seemed like ages, he emerged and handed a tray of food to the woman. She delved into her bag, searching for her purse. Why hadn't she got the money ready? Anna wondered, getting more and more annoyed. Then the woman looked behind her, calling out to someone further back. Not enough cash — more waiting! Anna swore in Polish.

Why were things always like this here? Anna looked over at Cassie and waved again. Another hour, that was all, and then she could hand the child back to her mother.

A group of teenagers stopped in front of her and began to chat and check their phones. Now Anna couldn't see their table clearly. She stepped to the side so she could see Cassie, and promptly lost her place in the queue. This was beyond a joke. She stamped her foot and swore again, prompting a series of angry looks from the others queuing beside her. She ranted at the teenagers in Polish, and even shook her fist at them.

She'd had enough. This entire thing had been a waste of time. Still livid, she crossed the few feet separating her from their table.

Cassie Rigby was gone.

* * *

"That went well, Thomas. I have to say you did her proud. Auntie Freda would be pleased with you." Fallon clapped his cousin on the shoulder. "And who is this?"

"Zoe. Zoe Calladine, my daughter."

"You and Rachel?" Well, I can certainly believe Rachel could produce such a lovely young woman; but you, Thomas?

"It's none of your damn business, Ray, so back off."

"Pleased to meet you, love." Fallon ignored his cousin and put out his hand. "How d'you find Leesdon then? Shithole, isn't it?" He chuckled, getting the full force of Calladine's foot on his shin for swearing.

"Forgive me, Zoe. Your father doesn't approve of me — poor sod never did, even when we were kids. Used to beat me black and blue, he did — bullying bastard."

Wasn't that the truth! And what a pity he couldn't take a serious pop at him now.

Fallon studied the young woman for a moment or two. "I'm not sure how much you know about your family but him and me, we're the only ones left. That being so, we should get to know each other better. I know Marilyn would love that. Marilyn's my wife," he explained. "We don't live around here, though. I got out — too bloody true I did. We live in Cheshire — got quite a pile, haven't we, Thomas?"

Calladine grunted his reply and made to lead Zoe away without looking at Fallon. But Zoe was having none of it.

"Thanks, Ray. I might just do that." She smiled.

"No, you damn well won't!" Calladine pulled Zoe towards the vicar, who was standing in the church doorway. "We'll say our goodbyes to Reverend Buckley and then get everyone to the hotel."

"You're very rude," Zoe told him. "He's your cousin. You were close once, so why don't you get on now? He can't be that bad."

She had no idea. And hopefully she'd never need to learn.

"We were never close and, no, we bloody well don't get on. I don't want you getting on with him either. The man's a murdering bastard. Don't be taken in; he's evil. At times, when I have no choice but to be in his company, like today, I'm forced to smile and pretend, but that's all it is. Do you understand?"

"Well, I still don't think you were very nice. You hardly spoke to him. In fact, you were positively glacial. He can't have felt welcome at all."

Calladine didn't give a toss about his cousin's finer feelings. And Fallon must have taken the hint because he and his goons were making for the Bentley.

Fallon called out to Thomas one last time, "Can't make the wake! But I've put a ton behind the bar, so have a drink on me."

Calladine's expression didn't change. Who did he think he was?

"That was very kind of him. He seems nice enough from where I'm standing, and wealthy too from the look of him."

Calladine would have liked to tell her just how he'd amassed all that wealth, but this wasn't the time or the place. Anyway, her mobile was ringing.

"You didn't turn yours off."

"It's as well I didn't. It's for you."

It was his sergeant, Ruth Bayliss. "We've got a missing child. I know this is a difficult day for you, and I wouldn't have rung if I'd had any choice in the matter, but she's only four. So you needed to know at once. One minute she's sat at a table in the garden centre café — the next she's gone. The childminder said it was as if she literally disappeared into thin air."

Ruth had been right to ring him. If no one had found her within a few minutes, then it was probable the child had been taken. His stomach churned. What sort of hell was in store for him now?

"Not had one of those in a while. Have you put out an alert?"

"Yes, and I'm waiting to see the parents. We need to interview them, get an up-to-date photo, and possibly even arrange a search of the house. As I said, the kid was with the childminder — a young woman called Anna Bajek. The parents, a Mr and Mrs Robert Rigby, were at work. I've contacted them and they're on their way home. I'm in the car outside the house now. Miss Bajek is still at the station, waiting to give a statement."

"Shouldn't you still be away? I thought that jaunt to Wales was four days," he asked, wondering why Ruth was working when she should be on leave.

"Ray, the chap who organises the birding group, has had an accident. The silly bugger fell off a ladder and broke his leg. So, of course, Joan had to drop out and that only left two of us so we shelved the trip until later in the year."

"Sorry about that. You were dead keen too. What was it, kites?"

"Yes, Tom, red kites, but no matter."

"Okay. Give me the address and I'll meet you there. Phone the nick; don't let the childminder go until I've spoken to her too."

"You can't leave. It's your own mother's funeral!" Zoe Calladine was angry.

"She's right, sir," Ruth piped up in his ear, overhearing what Zoe had said.

"It's fine. It's over now, bar the boozing, anyway.'

"Okay — but don't come unless you're sure. I can handle things for now."

He knew she could. Ruth Bayliss was a first-class sergeant. But they were already one man down and another of their number, DC Simon Rockliffe, was still on light duties. He'd received a head injury while investigating their last case and had only recently returned to work.

"I'm sorry." He took Zoe to one side. "We've a missing child — a very young child, too. I have no choice, surely you can understand that? This is what it's like with me, Zoe. This is the reason your mother and I stood no chance . . . I'll see you later. I'll try and get to the wake, but I can't promise. Look — the weather's filthy, why don't you do something about all those lovely flowers? They'll just go to waste if they're left lying out on the grave in this rain. Let Monika take some to the home. I'm sure your gran would approve." He smiled and kissed her cheek — then he was gone.

Chapter 2

Both parents were older than Calladine would have expected — possibly in their early forties. They were understandably distressed; and Mrs Rigby's anguish was only too evident. Sitting in an armchair, she was red-faced with crying, clutching a hankie to her face and trembling with emotion. Mr Rigby was not as visibly upset as his wife. Trying to hold things together for her sake? Delayed shock? There was always the possibility it was down to something else.

Whatever was going on inside his head, Robert Rigby seemed too much at ease, given what had just happened. He made a pot of tea and spoke about his daughter in a matter of fact way, almost as if he expected her to come running into the room at any minute. Once they sat down to talk, Mr Rigby handed Calladine a photo that had been sitting on the window sill. Cassandra Rigby was playing on a beach and smiling happily. She had curly blonde hair and a smattering of freckles across her cheeks.

"Does Miss Bajek look after Cassie often?" Ruth asked.

"Yes. She has her most days, except for the weekend."

"Is she trustworthy? Did she provide you with references?"

"This is all my fault, isn't it? I should have stayed at home until Cassie went to school next year. But I couldn't do that, could I? I had to have that damn shop, and now look what's happened."

Mrs Rigby broke down again. Her husband tried to comfort her, but she pushed him away.

"Anna came highly recommended by a friend. I'm sure she's absolutely fine, Inspector," said Mr Rigby.

"Nevertheless, we'll interview her and get a statement. How long has she been with you?"

"A few months. We have to have a childminder unfortunately. I work full time at the Council offices, and my wife has the florist shop in Leesdon. Anna occasionally has Cassie all day but mostly it's just for three or four hours. Being her own boss, Jane is able to juggle her hours, you see."

"What is it you do at the council, Mr Rigby?"

"I work in the Planning Department — all very boring and routine, I'm afraid." He smiled.

The Planning Department — could there be anything in that? Calladine wondered. People would go to extraordinary lengths to get what they wanted from town planners these days, particularly if it involved a housing development.

"I don't want this next question to upset you, but I have to ask it," Calladine told them. "Do you know of anyone who'd want to take Cassie? Has anyone threatened you or your family — anyone to do with your work for instance? Have you seen anyone hanging around — watching you all or taking a particular interest in your daughter?"

Both parents shook their heads.

"No one is interested in us personally, Inspector," Robert Rigby told them.

"Well there is that man, Alton." Jane Rigby spoke up. "You know — the one I told you about. I might be over-reacting but he scares me. He owns the nursery where I get some of my stuff. He was really off with me the other day. In fact he mentioned you, and it wasn't in a nice way either. He swore profusely and I did find his behaviour a little threatening."

Robert Rigby shrugged and shook his head. "There's nothing in that, Inspector. Just a run-of-the mill spat about acquiring some land, that's all." He turned to his wife. "You know how he is — how he feels about the buyout. Just an overreaction, no more than that."

"Nonetheless, perhaps you should tell me about it?" Calladine said.

"It's all very tedious really. Leesworth Council, in partnership with a housing association, want to build a number of small affordable homes. You know how expensive property is getting around here. The large tract of land at the back of the garden centre was identified as a possible site, but it won't be enough on its own, so the owner of Leesworth Plant Nursery, the adjoining property, was approached. I don't know if you've met him, but he's a very difficult man. Wanted nothing to do with it — refused absolutely to even consider the offer we made him. A very generous offer too. Relocation, compensation — the works."

"I take it he supplies plants to the garden centre, so he knows it well?"

Both parents nodded.

"I'd imagine so," Mrs Rigby added. "His stuff is really good. He's an excellent grower. I'm awaiting a delivery of potted hyacinths for Christmas as we speak."

"I'd be surprised if Cassie's disappearance has anything to do with him, Inspector. I can't really influence much at the Department — I'm not that important."

"Could there be anyone else; anyone with a grudge?"

"No one notices us, not really. We're just ordinary. We've no reason to draw attention to ourselves." Mrs Rigby's voice shook a little more with every word she spoke.

"Has Cassie ever wandered off before?" Ruth asked.

"No, never. She's a good little girl and she wouldn't go off anywhere on her own. She knows about not talking to strangers too."

"Would Cassie recognise the man from the nursery?"

Jane Rigby nodded and buried her head in her hands. This was getting them nowhere. Anything she might be able to offer was overshadowed by her emotion.

These cases were always heart-wrenching. Calladine looked around the sitting room. It was nicely furnished with good quality stuff. A large Christmas tree had pride of place in the front window, with a number of presents lying underneath it. If they didn't find the child soon, this was going to be hard.

"Okay. We'll arrange for a WPC to stay with you. We're already on with this, and she'll relay everything that's going on to you, particularly any progress we make. The minute we know anything, when we find Cassie, you'll be the first to know." Calladine handed Mr Rigby his card. "Ring me if anything happens, or should you be contacted."

"What do you mean?" Mrs Rigby raised her head. "You're talking blackmail, aren't you?"

Calladine looked at the woman. Why would she think that? She'd just said how ordinary they were, so why would she imagine they'd attract the attention of someone wanting money?

"I'm not thinking of anything in particular. In case anyone tries to pester you, notably the press, my advice is to tell them nothing — not yet. We will hold a press conference soon, and tell them what we want them to know. In cases like this they can sometimes help. Other agencies will be involved in finding Cassie too. You will hear from them. He watched the fear mount in her eyes.

"You think Cassie has been taken by some . . . some sort of pervert, don't you?"

Mr Rigby tapped her arm. "They don't think that, and you know as well as I do how unlikely that is. This is something else entirely, some silly mix up I'm sure. Remember what I told you." His look at her plainly indicated: *say no more*.

Odd thing to come out with. But emotion did strange things to folk.

"We don't think anything yet," was Calladine's reply to her question. "We're simply following procedure. We will work fast, and we'll do our best — that I can promise you."

* * *

"Is it just me, or is there something they're not telling us, sir?" Ruth asked, once they were outside. "She's obviously devastated, but he's something else. And did you hear that comment? What does he mean by 'silly mix up'? Does he imagine that one small child is very much the same as any other, and some poor woman has gone home with the wrong kid?"

Calladine raised his dark eyebrows. Ruth wasn't wrong. They were an odd couple. He couldn't quite put his finger on it, but something was going on there.

"I suppose we have to make allowances for the shock of what's happened. People are quick to imagine all sorts in circumstances like this."

"But how can he know she's not been taken?" Ruth argued. "Whoever owns that nursery will most certainly get a visit as soon as. But apart from that, Rigby's holding something back — I'll lay odds on it."

"Who's the WPC?"

"Kate Robinson. She's okay; she'll keep her ears peeled."

Kate was good at her job. Calladine knew that she had aspirations to become a detective too. He'd see how she went, what she could turn up about the Rigbys while she was there. They could do with replacing Dodgy as quickly as possible.

"You go back to the station and give the other agencies the heads up. You can start looking into that pair's background too. I want to know all about that family, the complete picture, and particularly since Cassandra was born. Follow up on the plant nursery too. I'll join you in a while." He checked his watch. "I'd better put in an appearance at the Leesworth Hotel — see if anyone's still hanging around. Then I'll call a team meeting. Get Imogen to check the garden centre for CCTV. You never know."

* * *

By the time Calladine got there, there were only a few mourners left at the hotel. Zoe was seated on a stool at the bar, deep in conversation with another young woman.

"I asked Jo to come and join me. You don't mind do you? You went off so quickly, and I'd no idea if you'd be back or not." She smiled. "I didn't want to sit here on my own." She nodded at a group of elderly folk sat around a table. "They're all lovely and have some wonderful tales to tell about Gran, but I fancied some company my own age."

He looked around at who was left. Monika hadn't stayed long then. He couldn't blame her. She'd be wary of having to make inane small talk with him.

"Did you sort the flowers with Monika?"

"Yep — she took some. She was very grateful."

"Good. Did she say anything else?" He almost hoped she'd asked about him.

"No, nothing important. Anyway, this is Jo Brandon. She owns the estate agents below the solicitors' office where I work."

Calladine nodded and offered to buy the two of them a drink. He was pleased Zoe was settling down and making friends, and this Jo seemed nice.

She offered her hand and a wide smile. "Pleased to meet you, Mr Calladine. Zoe's told me lots about you."

"That's not a local accent. You're a long way from home, I'd say."

"Guess I can't hide it, can I? Pennsylvania's my home, but I like it here."

"I can't stay long. As I said before, I've got a missing child, so I need to get on top of things fast. I'm sorry. I can't promise I'll be home any time soon either."

"That's okay, Tom. I'm not Mum, I do understand about your job, you know. I'm a solicitor, so I know about police work."

They'd agreed when Zoe first came into his life that she'd call him Tom. She'd had no problem with calling him dad, but the inspector didn't think he deserved the title — not yet anyway. He'd known her for such a short time, and he'd had no part in bringing her up. Perhaps in the future, once they both knew each other better and could see how things were going to pan out between them.

"How will you get back?"

"Jo will take me. In fact I might go back to hers and stay the night, so be as late as you like."

"We're waiting for the roads to clear," Jo said. "There was a nasty car crash earlier in the fog and the traffic's still bad."

"I didn't know — I didn't come that way."

"Why didn't you tell me about your cousin?" Zoe asked, changing the subject. "I don't understand why you wouldn't, because you've precious few blood relatives."

"I didn't tell you because he's a hoodlum, and I don't like him, not one little bit, that's why." He saw Jo smirk. "Despite what you might think, he's a damned embarrassment. You've seen him once. I've had to live with him, remember? And that wasn't easy."

"He can't be that bad, surely. You've so little family. Have you never considered trying harder?"

"Not with him I haven't. I'm not spinning you a tale, Zoe. Ray Fallon is evil. He's utterly ruthless and doesn't give a damn who he hurts, and that includes family. So keep away. I don't want you involved with him or his wife, poor cow that she is."

"Well, that's telling me. My mum always used to say you were a hard man. Now I see what she meant."

"Hard — perhaps. But only when a situation demands it. I'm not stupid, though, and getting involved with Fallon would be just that — plain stupid."

Zoe walked her father to the hotel entrance. "Drive carefully. This fog is hanging about, and it could come down thick again later."

"Ditto. Are you and Jo planning a night out? Leesworth isn't that bad. There are one or two really nice pubs."

"We might. We'll see how things go. But I think we'll probably just go back to hers and chill. You know, order a curry and watch some telly, nothing special."

It sounded glorious. What he'd give to have the same opportunity. Some downtime would suit him right now, particularly after the funeral.

"As long as you're happy, love."

Zoe waved, watching him drive away down the bleak, grey road. It hadn't really got light properly today, and no doubt the fog would close in again once it got dark. It would be a long, cold night.

* * *

"Doc Hoyle wants you to ring him, sir," Imogen called out as Calladine entered the main office. "D'you know about the smash this morning?"

"Yeah, I heard."

"He's looking very dapper," Rocco noted, as the DI hurried past his desk.

"His mother's funeral, idiot. So tread carefully, he's bound to be delicate for a while."

"He does look good though. He's a very attractive man under that stoic exterior. We tend not to notice — him being the boss," said Joyce, the admin assistant.

Imogen smiled in reply. She wondered if Joyce had the hots for their inspector. If she did, she'd kept it quiet for long enough, dark horse that she was.

Calladine went to his office and discarded his overcoat. He felt uncomfortable in his black suit and tie. He loosened the thing from around his neck and went to check what they'd got.

"CCTV?" he fired at Detective Constable Imogen Goode.

"Yes, sir, but there's not a lot to see. The camera's positioned above the till facing the café, but it only captures a small area. It's specifically for checking on till security, nothing else."

"Witnesses?"

"Details were taken by the manageress, a Mrs Sandra Dobson. She's good; she took the names and addresses of everyone in the place before she'd let them go. I'll get on to it, but it'll take some time."

"We could do with more bodies to help. Perhaps Long's team can do some of the legwork."

"I'm looking into the Rigbys' background," Ruth said. "And like I thought, there's definitely something odd about that pair . . ."

She didn't have time to explain more, because Joyce called out to him. "Doctor Hoyle, sir." She held out the phone.

"Doc! To what do I owe this pleasure?"

"I could do with seeing you, Tom, and pretty quick."

"Something up?"

"I think there might be, yes. I've been presented with a bit of a puzzle from the pile-up this morning."

"There were fatalities, then? I didn't realise it'd been that bad. How many are we talking about?"

"There were two fatalities, Tom. There was one at the scene, and one later at the hospital. And there is also my little conundrum."

"Want to expand on that, Doc?"

"No. I think it's better if I show you."

Doctor Sebastian Hoyle, senior pathologist at Leesdon General, was being cryptic again. But if he wanted to see him, then it had to be something important.

"See you soon, then."

"Ruth! Fancy a trip to the morgue?"

"The details of the missing girl have gone out, sir," she told him, picking up a pile of paperwork from her desk. "You've still got Anna Bajek waiting to be interviewed, remember?"

He'd forgotten. "Look — can you talk to her while I go see what the doc wants?"

Chapter 3

"She most certainly didn't die in the pile-up, Tom. You only have to look at her to see that. In fact, she's been dead in excess of forty eight hours," Hoyle said.

"How did she die, then?" Calladine replied.

"Well, not from natural causes, that's for sure."

Calladine followed the pathologist into his post-mortem room. The body of a young woman, covered in a white sheet from the chest down, was laid out on the table. Apart from the burnt flesh, it was obvious that she'd died from a catastrophic wound to the neck.

But what immediately struck Calladine was her mouth. Her lips had been crudely sewn together with string.

"No more than twenty-one, five foot three and very thin. I've still to do the PM and I will check for signs of bulimia. If that's the cause, then it should show up, but it could be she's simply been starved."

Calladine stared at the young woman in silence. The wounds around each of the puncture marks, made by what must have been a pretty hefty needle, had swollen hideously. Not done post-mortem then. Who could do such a thing? Who would choose to inflict such pain?

"Did she have any identification?"

"Not really. Nothing with a name and address on it anyway. She was exactly as you see her, stark naked and no jewellery. I've cut away one of the stitches and most of her front teeth have been broken or removed too." He inhaled sharply. "Unless we get something from DNA or fingerprints, then we've nowhere to go, I'm afraid."

"In that case we're looking at murder. What caused the wicked looking neck injury?"

"It looks highly likely that she was garrotted, Tom. Whoever did this exerted so much force, with whatever was used, that it cut right through her trachea. I'll look at the wound closely during the PM, but I'd say wire was the culprit."

Poor girl. She was so young, so fragile-looking — just a few years younger than Zoe in fact. And like Zoe, she'd had all her life in front of her. What sort of maniac does this — destroys youth and innocence with such lack of feeling? Calladine shuddered. This bastard needed catching before he got a taste for it.

"Look at this." Hoyle lifted one of her hands. "She's been bound, or even chained. The brown marks around her wrist look like rust to me, but I'll get Julian to check." He was talking about Julian Batho, the lead forensic scientist. "The same marks are around her ankles." He inhaled deeply again and pursed his lips. "I shouldn't speculate, Tom, but it has all the hallmarks of torture, even at this early stage. Taking a guess, I'd say she'd been kept chained up, tortured over time, and then killed. Plus there's this." Hoyle removed the sheet to expose her abdomen

Her lower belly was badly bruised, and there was dried blood on the inside of her inner thighs.

"Her pelvis is broken in several places. You see the marks? Several heavy blows with a blunt instrument I'd say."

Calladine flinched. This was the stuff of nightmares.

"Sexual assault?"

"It looks that way, but again, the PM will tell me more. But she certainly had intercourse shortly before death, because there is semen present. I'd say the experience wasn't pleasant. From the bruises I'd say she's been raped repeatedly."

This wasn't a crime carried out in the heat of an argument. This had taken time. Her death had been dragged out, made as painful as possible. And whoever had done this to the poor girl could well be planning to do it again.

The doctor moved her long fair hair to one side to show the inspector what looked like some sort of livestock tag hanging from her earlobe.

"Although it's much thicker, it's been fitted rather like a pierced earring, and there is even a number on it: the number five. On the reverse is a word, but I can't quite make it out, or understand what it means."

Calladine hoped that 'five' wasn't an indication of her place in some nutter's hit list.

"What word?"

"Well, I'll clean the thing up and get the microscope on it, but for now it looks like *Vida*."

Calladine shook his head. The word meant nothing to him either.

"I'll let you have the results pretty fast, later today, except for the DNA. I'll do DNA testing on the girl and the semen and I'll get it rushed through."

Just what he needed — a missing child, and now this. "Do we know which car she was in?"

"She was lying across the rear seat of a car which had one of the badly injured in it. A man — got all his details. His legs were injured in the smash, and then the car caught fire. He was unconscious when they got to him — smoke inhalation. The fire crew got there in time to put the fire out, so he was damned lucky if you ask me."

"I'll need his details."

Hoyle handed him an interim report. "There was a briefcase, and I've handed that over to Julian's people."

"Thanks, Doc. I'll speak to him before I leave. See what he remembers."

* * *

As he left the mortuary, Calladine took his mobile from his coat pocket.

"Ruth, how did you get on with the childminder?"

"She's pretty cut up about what happened, sir. I took her statement and then got her a lift home. She checks out. The recommendation for the job with the Rigbys was from a local GP. I rang him and he spoke very highly of her. She blames herself. From what she told me, the child was gone in an instant."

"There's been another incident, so get Imogen to look at what you've got on the Rigbys. Then come to the hospital, and I'll fill you in on what we've got here — something rather nasty, I'm afraid."

"To do with Cassie Rigby?"

"No — to do with the body found in the pile-up this morning."

Ruth had no idea what he was talking about, but she recognised the tone. Whatever had taken him away in such a rush was obviously big.

DS Ruth Bayliss arrived within ten minutes. Calladine was waiting for her by the entrance, holding two polystyrene cups of coffee. As she walked across the tarmac towards him he noticed something different about her. It had been niggling him for a while, and he couldn't work out what it was. She'd grown her hair a little longer, had things done to the colour, but that wasn't it. There was something else. For now, he'd just put it down to the 'Jake Ireson' effect and keep an eye on her.

"What's this all about, sir? Haven't we got enough on with the Rigby case?"

"This is a murder, Ruth, and a particularly brutal one at that. If my instincts are right, there may be others." He handed her one of the cups, looking grim. "It has all the hallmarks of a really evil bastard — holding her captive, torture and sexual assault — way over the top. And her mouth has been mutilated — some of her teeth were removed and her lips were stitched together with string. String! Can you believe that? She wouldn't have been able to talk, eat or even drink, the way she was left. So you tell me — what do we do? Shelve it until Cassie Rigby turns up, or crack on?"

His lurid description made Ruth shiver. "Where was she found?"

"Her body was in one of the cars. The driver has just come out of surgery."

"Perhaps this isn't so complicated after all then, sir. And you're absolutely sure that she can't have got the injuries in the crash?"

"Please — after what I've just told you, what do you think? And anyway, to finish her off, she was garrotted."

His tone was sombre. Calladine didn't like this one. It was giving him that feeling again, one he hadn't had since the *Handy Man* case.

"So you think this guy planned to dump the body somewhere and got caught in the pile-up instead?"

"I don't think anything. For a start, no attempt had been made to hide her, and she was stark naked. You'd imagine the boot would be a better place to hide a naked body, wouldn't you?"

Ruth Bayliss didn't know what to think. "This gives us a huge caseload, and we're short on the team. The missing child and now this; it's going to really stretch us."

Calladine scratched his head. It couldn't be helped. Things were what they were.

"With regard to Cassie Rigby, sir, shouldn't we alert Central? Perhaps we should be treating it as a Category A incident from the off. Child abduction is big time and we're delaying things."

"No, we're not. We'll get the preliminaries done first. You met those people; something's not right in that house. We need to get to the bottom of it, because it's more than likely pivotal to the child's disappearance. Look, I'm sorry things have got so hectic suddenly, but you know how it is. If you'd anything planned, then apologies. You'll just have to make Jake see how things are," Calladine said.

"He'd promised to take me to that new Italian place in Hopecross. So — yes, I was hoping for an early dart, but he'll understand. He'll have to."

Calladine knew how hard it was — combining a private life with the job. He also knew that Ruth had been seeing her teacher since they met during a previous investigation. Things were at what she liked to call 'the interesting stage.' From this point on, their relationship would settle into something more permanent, or else it would fold. But one way or another, a relationship demanded compromises if it was to succeed. Calladine was a good example of what happened if you didn't.

They went to find the injured man.

"You like him, then?"

"Yes, I suppose I do, but it's not easy. I've lived alone for so long it causes problems. Then there's the job. It's a minefield, it really is."

Wasn't that the truth?

* * *

"He's still groggy," the nurse told them, as the two detectives arrived on the ward.

"What's the damage?" Calladine spoke to a young doctor hovering over the semi-conscious man.

"Broken femur — we've fixed it with a nail and some screws, plus superficial burns and smoke inhalation. He'll be hoarse, don't expect too much. He's had a heavy dose of morphine so he might not know what you're even talking about."

Alexander Stone was a rep for a clothing company based in Liverpool.

"Mr Stone . . ." Calladine shook his arm gently. "Do you remember anything about this morning?"

The man looked to be in a bad way. His face was crimson from the fire and his leg was bandaged. He was muttering. Nothing coherent, Calladine thought, as he put his ear closer to the man's mouth. Just rubbish. That'd be the drugs.

But Alexander Stone was conscious, barely, and turned his head to look at who was bothering him.

"Bloody mess." He coughed and spluttered. "Bastard terrified me . . ." The coughing took over again.

"Do you remember the woman?"

He screwed up his face and shook his head. "What woman? I travel alone. There was no woman — not with me anyway."

His eyes closed and he visibly relaxed onto the pillow as the drugs finally won the battle. The nurse stuck the oxygen mask on his face and shrugged.

'You won't get anything else I'm afraid. I suggest you come back in a few hours, or even better, tomorrow.'

So that was that. The two detectives left the ward and strode down the corridor to the lift.

"I'll have a word with Julian before we leave," Calladine decided. "He has Stone's briefcase. I want to know where he's been these last few days and what he was doing on the bypass this morning. I don't think he's anything to do with this, because it doesn't add up. It's the way the woman's body was just lying there on the back seat for anyone to see, and in that state too. It's bugging me. I'll meet you back in the car park."

"The body was in Stone's car so he must have put her there. He's our man — straightforward enough, so why make things more difficult? Don't we have enough to think about?"

Calladine watched her walk off shaking her head. He knew what she thought — he was at it again, joining up dots that weren't there.

* * *

"Julian, did Stone have a diary, electronic or otherwise, in that case of his?" Calladine poked his head around the lab door. "Also — something occurs to me. The car with the body in it, can you determine if it caught fire on its own, or if there was an accelerant used?"

Julian Batho raised his head from a mass of paperwork, and gave the inspector one of his enigmatic little smiles.

"Got a theory, DI Calladine? Looking for more than meets the eye — again?"

"Usually right though, aren't I? So less of the sarcasm please, Julian. Just let me know what you find, as soon as. Oh — and let me have a diagram that shows the position of the other vehicles, relative to the car you found her in."

Julian Batho reached across his desk and handed Calladine a tablet computer. "It's all on there — his diary, appointments, everything. There's no password. Get Imogen to look at it for you."

Calladine nodded his thanks. He met Ruth outside the room.

"What's going on in your head, sir? Imogen's been on the phone: DCI Jones has been looking for you, and Long's team are up to their eyes with something big of their own. Things seem cut and dried to me. So we need to sort the missing kid thing urgently — don't you think?"

"I'm not looking to make work for us, Ruth. We've got a murder on our hands. Whichever way you look at it and, regardless of what you think, I'll lay odds that Stone isn't our man."

Chapter 4

Day Two

Calladine was busy removing the remains of an old case from the incident board. "Right folks — gather round. Let's get this up and running. We're dealing with two unconnected cases; a missing child and a suspicious death. Although I haven't yet got the post-mortem report I can safely say that this young woman was brutally murdered." He pinned a photo to the board. "There are one or two things that want doing urgently, so as to rule suspects in or out. We should be able to rule out Alexander Stone very soon. He was driving the car she was found in, but I don't think he had anything to do with it." The team exchanged looks and began to whisper. "Yes, I know what some of you are thinking, but bear with me for a little while longer."

"All his appointments are in his electronic diary, sir." Imogen held up a tablet for the team to see. "Everyone he's seen for the past twelve months."

Rocco piped up. "I hear what you say, but doesn't finding the body in his car make it a little obvious who the killer is? His car; his crime. What other explanation could there be?"

"It just doesn't feel right. He takes time destroying her, doing the most appalling things to her, then shoves her in his car — naked and uncovered, just laid across the back seat for all to see."

"He's a nutter; they panic sometimes."

"We'll see. I've asked Julian to do some tests; then we'll know for sure. Until then we won't make any assumptions."

"Will you make a list of his appointments for the last fortnight?" he asked Imogen. "Then we can each take a few and check them out. Now — the murdered girl." He shook his head. "Someone did a right job on her — the sort of job that takes time and shouts psychopath."

Imogen Goode heard the *ping* of new mail, and her blue eyes dipped to her computer screen. There was a message from Julian.

"Sorry to interrupt, but Julian says you want this urgently, sir." She was already sending the document to the printer.

It was the diagram Calladine had requested, and as he'd thought, Stone's vehicle was the last one in the pile-up. He pinned it to the board. It was an important piece in the jigsaw.

He turned back and looked at the team. Where was Ruth? He glanced up at the office clock — nine thirty. Way past her usual time. Well, he couldn't wait for her.

"This young woman was found dead in a car on the bypass this morning. She definitely wasn't killed in the smash. She'd been murdered somewhere else — garrotted. There is more, and you'll all get a copy of the PM report once Doc Hoyle has written it. It won't make pleasant reading. Our man did a thorough job. Stone was stuck in his car, unable to move, and no doubt screaming for help. No-one could see anything because of the fog. Even though she was found in his car, it's my theory that it went like this: another vehicle comes up behind him and stops. This vehicle has the dead girl in it. Stone probably thinks he'll get some help, but that's not what happens. The bastard ignores him and dumps the girl's body on his rear seat. Next, he tries to cover it up by setting the car alight."

He stood back, staring at the board. If he was right, then their man must have had no idea what to do with the body. He'd simply seized an opportunity when it had presented itself. That could mean she was his first.

"Like I said, that last bit is only a theory at present. But if I'm wrong then we have to ask ourselves why Stone didn't hide her? I've got Julian's lot checking to see if his car was set alight deliberately. If it was, then our man was hoping to cover his tracks. Stone's car was the obvious choice — an incapacitated driver and the first car he came across in the heavy fog." He tapped at the diagram. "I'm not going to pretend; this isn't going to be easy. We're short-staffed, and what with this and the Cassie Rigby case, we're overstretched. Rocco: you and Imogen take the kid for now. Ruth and I will look into the murdered girl."

As he uttered her name, Ruth Bayliss entered the incident room. She was flustered and looked pale and tired. Putting her coat over a chair back, she nodded at Calladine and sank wearily onto a seat.

"If the Cassie Rigby case turns into something big, then the investigation will escalate and we'll get more bodies on the job. But we'll finish all the preliminary checks first. We have to treat this as a simple case of a missing child — if there is such a thing — until we know different. I want all the different agencies kept up to speed with what we find."

* * *

Ruth hadn't had the best of starts this morning; yet another row with Jake. The man could be so unreasonable. What he wanted was a woman who kept regular hours, who worked nine to five, then went home and fixed tea.

But what he'd got was Ruth and her job. He even had the nerve to turn his nose up at her hobby — birdwatching. It took her away with a bunch of people he didn't know, and some of them were men. How stupid was that?

Jake didn't understand her passion for ornithology, or, given her job, how little time she had to devote to it. Now she'd have Calladine on her back for being late, and she could hardly blame him.

But it wouldn't take her long to get her brain into gear. She wasn't sure if the boss was right. How could a missing child ever be a simple case? Something had happened to Cassie Rigby, and if they didn't find her soon, then Calladine could have a lot to answer for. She swept her dark hair away from her face in irritation, and resolved to get it cut at the first opportunity. She'd only grown it because Jake had said it suited her. Stupid vain female that she'd become all of a sudden — all because of a man. Not like her at all.

Imogen Goode, however, seemed only too pleased to be handed more responsibility, whether the boss was right or not. She smiled at Rocco and nodded. She had already made some headway, having looked over Ruth's research from the previous day.

"There's something odd going on. For a start, there is no record of Cassie Rigby's birth," she told Ruth. "In fact, there's no record of Mr and Mrs Rigby ever having had any children at all — weird don't you think?"

Yes, it was, but why didn't it surprise her? Right from the off, Ruth and Calladine had suspected that there was more to this than met the eye.

"Check to see if Cassie was born before they got married — look under Mrs Rigby's maiden name. If that draws a blank, then you'll have to go and ask them — and don't let them spin you any tales. The boss and I got the impression they had something to hide, so push them. Check with the garden centre too — ask if any of the staff saw the child leaving. If she didn't want to go with whoever took her, then she would have kicked up a fuss and someone would have heard."

"Do we know who she was, sir?" Ruth turned her attention to the murdered girl. The description Calladine was busy writing on the board looked awful. If he was right, the murder needed sorting every bit as much as the Cassie Rigby case.

"Not a clue. All we have is something written on a livestock tag attached to her ear — the word *Vida.*" He wrote the word on the board. "Is it a name, a place, or what? I've no idea."

A livestock tag. Ruth shuddered, her eyes widening.

"I'll check the HOLMES database and see if anything comes up." Imogen sat on the edge of Rocco's desk. "We'll visit the nursery first. We can take a look at the garden centre while we're there as well. Robert Rigby had a row with the nursery owner about the council wanting to buy his land," Imogen explained to Ruth. "Robert Rigby works in planning so there could be something in it — we'll see."

"Ruth!" Calladine beckoned his sergeant into his office.

He'd be wanting to talk, she guessed, about her arriving late. It wasn't her style.

"Come in and close the door behind you. Are you okay? You don't look right — I'm worried about you. What's going on?" Calladine asked.

"I've been a bloody fool, Tom." She sank into a chair facing him. "Jake. I got in too deep, and now . . . I'm floundering. I just don't know what to do."

This wasn't an overstatement. Ruth had been awake most of the night, tossing the alternatives about in her head. She liked Jake, but was that enough? Was it 'like,' or was it something more, and if it was, how would she know?

"Believe me, Ruth, where romantic cock-ups are concerned I'm a walking nightmare. You only have to look at the mess I'm in with Monika . . . But I don't understand what your problem is. He likes you, you like him. Why not just go for it?"

"Because so much would change, that's why. I suppose I'm frightened. I've lived alone for so many years — with no one to please but myself, and, despite what he says, he'd never understand the job. Let's face it, teaching is a cushy number compared to what we do. Most of the time I'd be here and he'd be at home. That'd only last so long. Look what happened to you and Rachel."

"It takes a special sort of person to put up with the life a detective leads, and Rachel didn't cope — not at all."

"I don't know if Jake would either, so I'm not sure I want the aggro of even trying." She pulled a face. "Late nights, stuff going on in my head — I'd be a nightmare to live with. He'd only go along with it for so long then it'd all be over anyway."

"Well, you have to make a decision because it's interfering with your work. This isn't me coming down hard — you're a friend as well as a colleague — but there is only so far I can let this go. I need my sergeant firing on all cylinders — particularly just now. So make up your mind. Go for it; he's a good man. And try and get that break — take Jake with you."

"Birdwatching! He wouldn't know a puffin from a parakeet."

Ruth smiled at him. She was getting the Calladine pep talk. It'd been a while, and it was more usual these days for her to be the one giving him guidance on how to live his life. Given the mess he made of his love life there was an irony there somewhere.

"I'll see. I'll have to think about it a bit longer." She took the diagram he held out to her. Back to work.

"Do you see what I mean about the car? If Stone had killed her, he'd have hidden her body; he wouldn't have left her naked like that on the back seat."

"Perhaps he panicked, didn't know what to do, and simply wanted rid."

"She'd been dead a while, so no, he didn't panic. She'd been kept somewhere, bound or chained. The bastard took his time with her. He damaged her teeth — I can only suppose it was meant to hinder identification. And look what he did to her mouth. Goodness knows how long he kept her like that. There's strong evidence of repeated sexual assault too. It's a bad one, Ruth. On the reverse of the thing in her ear lobe is the number five. It could mean anything, but we should hope she isn't part of some disturbing sequence and that there aren't more like her out there."

"I'll check missing persons, sir." She began making notes, taking down the preliminary description of the girl. "She's young too. I wonder if she's local, although I don't know the name — if that's what it is. We have a reasonable photo? Something we can show around? I suppose eventually there'll be a press conference, and then we can release it."

Calladine scowled at this. He didn't like the press. He didn't like the way they operated — how they transformed everything into something lurid and scandalous. "Only when we need to — not before. We could be wasting our time with the local newspaper anyway. She could be from anywhere. Whoever left her in the back of that car could have travelled. We just don't know."

Chapter 5

This was DC Simon 'Rocco' Rockliffe's first proper investigation since the *Handy Man* case, and he was nervous. What had happened to him that night in the tower block hadn't only left a dent in his skull, it had left a dent in his confidence too. Still, Imogen knew what she was doing. She was a natural, and Rocco knew he could trust her to mind his back.

He drove them both along the bypass and on towards the garden centre. He didn't say much.

The place was busy, all done up for Christmas.

"I must get a tree," Imogen declared, as they passed a row of Nordmann firs on the way in. "They make such a good show here, don't you think? The trees and all the sparkly lights — I think they've even got a Santa's Grotto this year too."

"Where was the girl sitting?" Rocco's expression was anxious. He didn't want to make small talk; he was on edge. He needed to achieve something positive, get back in the saddle.

Imogen had a quick word with Sandra Dobson, the manageress, and ordered two coffees. She took Rocco's arm.

"Relax. Don't stress so much, we'll do this, and then go back and report in."

Rocco gave her a weak smile. She'd want him to be more like the Rocco of old, to relax and joke. Trouble was, he still felt nothing like his old self, and he was beginning to wonder if he ever would.

"They were sitting over here. The girl was left on this very seat while Anna Bajek went to the counter over there. As you can see — she would have been quite visible. Now, according to Anna's statement, a group of school kids came in — half a dozen or more and they stood against that rail over there, in front of the counter. So for a short while Anna couldn't see Cassie at all."

"A very short while, according to her statement — literally seconds."

"Yes — so you know what that means?"

"It means they were being watched."

"My thoughts exactly. Someone was waiting for an opportunity to pounce. Perhaps they were followed here after they finished shopping on the High Street. When we get back to the nick we should check the CCTV."

Sandra Dobson brought the coffees over. "Have you got anything yet?"

"No — afraid not. But it's only been a few hours. We'd like to speak to your staff — see if anyone recalls seeing the child being taken away," Imogen replied.

"I've already asked, love. We were just too busy, so I'm afraid no one noticed anything out of the ordinary. But I'm sure that if a child had been taken out of here screaming and shouting, then someone would have come forward by now."

"Do you see much of your neighbour at the nursery?" Rocco asked.

"Not really; not unless he's bringing stock across or looking for Jonathan. James Alton isn't a particularly sociable animal."

"Jonathan?"

"My son. He works here and at the nursery. He fills in where he's needed." She pointed towards a young man serving at the counter. If I remember rightly, he was actually serving at lunchtime today. That's right, isn't it, Jonathan? You saw the woman and the kid?"

The young man nodded. "Can't say I remember much though. We were far too busy."

"Was James Alton in here earlier, when the girl went missing?"

"I didn't see him, but there's been no delivery from him today, so no, probably not, but I'll ask the rest of the staff."

"That's okay, we'll go and see him shortly."

Sandra Dobson left them to it.

"You okay, Rocco? You look a little tense," Imogen asked Rocco.

"I just need to get back into it, that's all, get stuff sorted in my head. I used to be so sure of myself, fearless almost, but now . . ." he shrugged, sipping on the hot coffee. "I'm in danger of being scared of my own shadow."

Imogen rubbed his arm. "You're going to be fine. We do a job — mostly it's okay but we're all aware that it can get hairy at times. You were unlucky. That woman lashed out and you got it. It could have been any one of you that night."

She was right — wrong place, wrong time.

"Have you missed me? I've been bored stiff. I might have become a bit of a wimp, but I'm still glad to be back."

"We've all missed you, Rocco. We've missed your cheeky face and banter about the office." She smiled, and gave him a wink. "And we've missed your input. It's no fun being short-handed."

"But you coped — the team always does." He smiled. "And there've been changes. What's with the inspector getting a daughter suddenly?"

"I know, and she's okay too. He found out about her the night you got injured. He had no idea. She simply turned up out of the blue and announced who she was — took him completely by surprise."

"Something's changed with you, too. You look a little different." He grinned. "But I can't work out what it is."

"Oh it's simple enough — I ditched the specs in favour of contact lenses." She smiled back at him. "Nothing major, but you'd be surprised what it does for a girl's confidence."

They laughed. Rocco would never have thought that the gorgeous blonde detective constable would have been short on confidence, specs or no specs.

"Is it for Julian's benefit?"

"No — and you stop that now." She slapped his chest playfully with the back of her hand. "Julian's just a friend. He's clever and I admire his work, nothing more. There was a time when I fancied forensic science myself."

He gave her a doubtful look — forensic science or the forensic scientist? There was no way Julian considered himself just another one of Imogen's friends. She was kidding herself if she thought that's how it was with him.

* * *

But they had a job to do, and so a short while later the two detectives were walking along the narrow grassy path that formed a short cut between the garden centre and the nursery. As it came into view, Imogen could understand why a house builder would want the land. It was a very large, flat area and convenient for both Leesdon and the bypass. The fact that James Alton wouldn't sell must have really pissed the council off.

There was a tall wooden gate at the end of the path, and it was unlocked — nothing to stop them then. The land had been divided up into six areas of similar size. It looked pretty desolate at this time of year. The sign by the gate said the nursery specialised in roses and fruit trees.

But now, in the harsh December weather, they were nothing but twigs in the frozen soil.

Each sectioned-off area had its own long, modern greenhouse, in sharp contrast to a block of old stone outbuildings that stood on the far perimeter of the land. Alton had obviously invested both time and money into his business.

The place looked empty. There was no one around and the first greenhouse they came too was padlocked shut.

Imogen called out, "Anyone here?"

There was no reply.

"There's a carport round the side but no vehicle, and the main gates back there are shut," Rocco said, he'd had a quick look round. "Perhaps he's out delivering — it's a busy time of year."

"It's quite a lonely spot, don't you think? You can't even see the garden centre from here, not with those conifers in the way. In fact, a lot of stuff could go on here, and no one would ever know."

"Imagination, DC Goode." Rocco grinned. "Don't get carried away."

"Do you think we dare check out the other buildings while we're here? It's not as if we have a search warrant or anything."

"We can always say we're looking for Alton." Rocco made off down a gravel path running along the side of one of the tracts of land. "Come on, then — I'll take these greenhouses, and you take the ones over there."

The two detectives got nowhere. All the buildings were locked up tight and there was no sign of any work going on.

"What the hell do you think you're doing?" A voice bellowed out from behind them. "How did you get in here? This is private land. Can't you read?" While they'd been busy looking around, the nursery van had pulled into the carport, and now a man was hurrying towards them. James Alton, Imogen presumed.

He was a tall, slightly overweight middle-aged man with a weather-beaten face that was set in a hard expression. Not a happy individual from the look of him.

"If you're from the damn council then you're wasting your time. The best I'll do for now is think about it. I won't be rushed, so stop hassling me!" He strode towards them.

Imogen flashed her warrant card and smiled at the man. "James Alton?"

"What of it?" His face was pulled into a stubborn frown.

"DC Goode and DC Rockliffe from Leesworth CID. We got in through the wooden gate back there. It wasn't locked."

"Bloody Jonathan. I keep telling him, but does he listen?"

"Can we ask you a few questions, Mr Alton?"

"Be quick. I don't have time for idle chit-chat."

"This is definitely not chit-chat, idle or otherwise, Mr Alton. We're looking for a missing child. She was in the garden centre café earlier today." Imogen showed him a photo of Cassie Rigby. "We wondered if you saw anything, anything odd or suspicious. Did anyone cross your land, trying to make for the road, for example?"

"No. If you opened your eyes and looked a little closer, you'd see that my boundary fence is nearly eight foot tall. So there's no way out, not this way."

"Could anyone hide in one of your buildings?"

"No. They're locked. They're always locked."

He was neither helpful nor friendly. He didn't once crack a smile, and seemed determined to say as little as possible.

"Mr Alton, can you account for your movements today?" Rocco was fed up with the man's tone.

James Alton sighed and led the way back to his van. He leaned in and retrieved a clipboard from the passenger seat. "The deliveries I've made today and the suppliers I've seen." He handed a bundle of notes to Imogen. "I'm busy now so take them away and return them when you've done." With that, he turned and left them standing beside the van as he strode towards one of his greenhouses.

"He could do with working on his interpersonal skills," Imogen commented. "A bit of civility costs nowt." She looked at the motley scraps of paper in her hand, and put them carefully into her shoulder bag.

Chapter 6

He took one last look in the full-length mirror — perfect, even if he did say so himself. Sharp as a blade — knockout in fact. What woman could resist him? Hopefully not her, he thought, picking up the photo he'd printed out from Facebook.

He smiled and gave his deep-blue silk tie one last tug. His suit was a few shades darker than the tie, and his shirt was dazzling white. He was young and tall and women found him attractive, so he played on his looks, using them to his advantage.

The girl was lovely, exactly what he was looking for. She was so like Vida it hurt. Could she be the one? She had to be; he'd spent enough time on that damn computer looking for her. All that time spent grooming her, followed by the endless chat, while he took care to give nothing away. He had the process of smooth talking his quarry into trusting him down to a fine art. And it would finally pay off tonight. He folded the photo neatly and placed it in the inside pocket of his suit jacket. No more delays; no more setbacks. He wanted things to move on. He needed a woman. He needed a woman's soft eager body in his bed, or fastened down on his chair. He closed his eyes as the images flooded his mind. He needed Vida — he'd always needed Vida. The problem was, she'd never needed him.

His face contorted into an ugly frown. This one would want him. If she knew what was good for her she would. If she didn't, if she resisted like all the others, then she'd suffer the same fate. He wouldn't tolerate refusal — he wouldn't listen to their pleas or their cries. He made sure he didn't have to. He gave a little flick with his hand, mimicking the way he drew the string hard through their lips. That way he made sure of winning every argument. That way he made certain he called all the shots. This one had better not get herself pregnant either. Two of the others had been stupid enough to get themselves up the duff. That had ruined everything. He'd tried to abort the pregnancies but nothing had worked. So in the end he'd had to get rid of the girls.

That would never happen with Vida, but if it did, he wouldn't mind. She could have whatever she wanted from him. She had the ability to dangle him on an imaginary chain while she teased and messed with his head. The bitch! But he still wanted her — the mind was a strange thing. He was far too soft for his own good. But where Vida was concerned, he couldn't help himself.

But tonight was a fresh start — another go at getting things right. Choose carefully and stay in the shadows. He wouldn't drive; he'd take the train. It was anonymous. The train from Leesworth Station would take him to Manchester Victoria, then he'd take the tram to St. Peter's Square. From there it was only a short hop down into student territory.

They'd agreed to meet in a bar — one she went to, along with other students. It'd be busy and noisy, with loud music blaring out. Nobody would notice him, not even dressed like this. They'd think he was off down Canal Street or to a smart club somewhere. No one would guess what he was really up to.

He was excited. A tense knot of nerves in his belly was making him nauseous — her fault. It was always like this with Vida. She had the effect of making his pulse race and his stomach churn. He'd make her pay. He always made her pay because he enjoyed it so much. He liked doing things to her — particularly the other things; those excruciatingly painful things. In the end she'd get the message. She'd behave and stop making him nervous. She'd have no choice.

The pub she'd suggested wasn't somewhere he'd normally go. It was a dark and dingy place that smelled of lager and smoke, which made him cough and wrinkle his nose in distaste. It sat under a railway arch, and although smoking was only allowed outside, it wafted in every time the door was opened. No place for a lady. No place for Vida. Why did she have to come here?

He looked around — the nerves were doing his head in. Her fault. Stupid bitch was doing it on purpose. He struggled through the throng of students, making for the bar, and then he saw her. She was sitting with another girl on a bench against the far wall, giggling and sipping on a beer. He snuck in behind a pillar and watched for a few moments. She was exactly like her photo, and exactly what he wanted. This one was a looker — but was she a perfect match for Vida? He'd have to wait and see; but as far as looks went, she was just how he liked them. He inhaled deeply — this was it. He allowed his mind to wander, just for a moment or two, and imagined her naked, in his special place, on his chair, and ready for him. Shit, he could feel the rush of blood to his loins and the flush on his cheeks. She'd be good — he just knew it.

"Patsy!" He smiled, striding up to her table. "Hope I haven't kept you waiting too long. Damn train was late."

"No worries, Jack." Patsy Lumis smiled back at him. "I've just been sitting here chatting with Anna."

She had the most wonderful American accent. Even better than he'd imagined.

"I thought we could go somewhere to eat," he offered. "Somewhere a bit quieter than here. I know a nice place in the Northern Quarter. How d'you fancy it?"

She shrugged and giggled at her friend. "What do you think? Should I go with him? Maybe you wanna come too? She smiled and looked up at Jack. "You wouldn't mind Anna coming with us, would you?"

What was wrong with her? Of course he'd bloody well mind! Couldn't she go anywhere alone — make a decision without a second opinion? He'd have to change that, even if he had to beat it out of her.

"You don't really want to do that, do you, Anna? You don't want to play gooseberry?"

His voice was firm. In fact it verged on the threatening.

Anna took the hint. She shook her head and reached across the bench for her bag. "You'll be fine, just be careful. Remember what we talked about, and text me," she instructed Patsy. "And don't be late back."

What was she — her fucking mother or something? He'd have to get Patsy away from her. She could be trouble — interfering bitch.

"She's just watching out for me," Patsy patted the place beside her where Anna had been sitting. "Come and sit down for. Have a drink, and then we'll go." She gave him a big smile.

That was what he needed — a stiff drink to calm his nerves. She was talking again, but he wasn't really listening to the words. It was her voice, that wonderful American accent. He loved it; just like Vida's voice. He loved the way she looked; but even better, he loved her white even teeth and those full pink lips — perfect. Particularly those lips. They'd look so good sewn together. He might try wire this time. He'd do it good and tight. Then she wouldn't answer him back.

She had that lovely long blonde hair he liked so much, and delicate features. There was even a spattering of freckles on her cheeks. He gulped with emotion; Vida got freckles in the summer.

Chapter 7

Day Three

Julian Batho marched into the main office and caught up with Calladine by the incident board.

"I think I might owe you an apology, Inspector."

"Not like you, Julian. What is it I've done to deserve one?" Calladine asked.

"You were right. Again." Julian grinned, raising his bushy eyebrows. "You see, I thought you were pushing it with the accelerant thing — but no, you were spot on."

Music to Calladine's ears.

"The accelerant used was petrol. The car ran on diesel."

"So the bastard did try to torch it?"

"Not my place, I know, but I'd say so. The petrol couldn't have run off from another car — there was nothing beside or behind it. Sorry I doubted your theory without checking first. It's just that you have this way of throwing stuff into the pot without any rhyme or reason."

"It's my instinct, Julian. I trust it and it's not let me down yet. Not that having you confirm what I suspected helps us much, because we still have a big fat nothing."

"We might have, sir." Ruth called out. "We can go and talk to Stone now. He's come round this morning, and is fit for interview." "Bet you're pleased the theory played out." She nudged him. "Not that it'll help much with the workload, but it does show that you're not losing your touch."

"Surprised you doubted me, Sergeant," he replied, pretending to be miffed. "We'll go and speak to Mr Stone now. We could get lucky. He might have seen something, remembered something that'll help us."

* * *

Calladine went to get his overcoat. On his way out he met DCI George Jones, his boss, who'd been looking for him.

"You're a difficult man to pin down. A word please, Tom." Jones looked annoyed.

Whatever had happened to piss off the DCI had obviously landed squarely at his feet. Calladine gestured to Ruth to wait, and followed him down the corridor into his office.

"There was a shooting in Manchester yesterday," began Jones, nodding for him to sit down. "The victim was a key witness in a murder and extortion racket. It was a professional job — a single shot through the left eye socket at close range."

Nasty, but what did it have to do with them? Surely this was one for Central? Calladine thought.

"The investigation, the evidence gathering — it ran over several months. Make no mistake, this was a major operation. The witness and his family were kept at a safe house under twenty-four hour guard. A lot of money was spent — and now all for nothing." Jones paused and frowned. "Central knows who did the shooting, Tom. There is only one name in the frame."

Calladine was still mystified. Surely this had nothing at all to do with him or the teams stationed at Leesworth.

"And that name gives me one huge problem, DI Calladine." Jones sighed. "Because he maintains you will provide him with a cast-iron alibi."

"You've lost me, sir."

"Can't you guess, Tom? Have you really no idea?" The DCI paused for a moment, giving Calladine time to think. "Your cousin, Ray Fallon. He took the witness from the safe house and shot him in cold blood. So you see my problem. I have to ask if he's asked you to lie for him."

Calladine was astonished that Jones could, even for a second, imagine that he knew anything about this.

"There's no way I'd ever provide an alibi for that murdering bastard, cousin or not," Calladine spluttered. "And I'm surprised you could even think that I would. He's got to be joking. When was this, sir?"

"The witness was killed between eleven and midday yesterday morning."

Tom Calladine shook his head and cursed. "Are you sure it was him? Fallon usually gets one of his people to do the dirty work."

"We've been led to believe that the information regarding the witness' whereabouts reached Fallon only yesterday morning," he shrugged, "so he did the job himself. You know he isn't averse to getting his hands dirty if he thinks he can get away with it — which he usually does."

That was why Fallon had come to the funeral. He'd used it and Calladine as a cover. He had no choice but to give Jones the bad news.

"In that case, he's telling the truth — and I'm not covering for him. We don't have much choice but to accept what he's saying. Ray Fallon was attending my mother's funeral at Leesworth Parish Church at that time. So not only me, but about thirty others can vouch for his presence."

"This doesn't sit well, Tom." Jones's face was like thunder.

How the hell did he imagine it sat with him!

"There's nothing much I can do about it, sir. He was there, along with a number of his goons. Even he can't be in two places at once."

"Central will want a word. In fact they'll want a statement. I don't like this, Tom. I don't like having one of my officers being involved with a gangster like Fallon."

"Let's get one thing clear, sir: I am most definitely not involved with him. The man's my cousin, so occasionally, when there's family stuff, like yesterday, I have to see him. But that's as far as it goes. I do not mix socially with him. I do not speak to him on the phone. In short — I have precious little to do with the man. Is that all, sir?"

"For now. But be warned: don't speak to Fallon at all — about anything. Do you understand?"

He certainly did. This was yet another nail in the coffin of his career.

"Can I ask, sir, how did they arrive at the exact time of death?"

"Post-mortem. He was dumped, and found almost straight away, so we got a reasonably accurate time of death."

"Why was that? Why was he found so soon?"

"Because about an hour after he was shot, the body was thrown from a bridge over the M62. The emergency services were at the scene within minutes. So there's no question."

"So what time does that put the shooting at?"

"The pathologist reckons about eleven."

"Even so I can't fault his alibi."

"Just bear in mind what I've said and keep away, Tom. Don't let me down."

So that was that. Fallon had well and truly stitched him up. He must have been laughing all through the service yesterday.

* * *

Ruth drove them to the hospital.

"You look tired, sir, case getting to you?"

"No, it's not the case. I've just had a run in with Jones about my bloody cousin. The bastard's dragged me into a damn murder case now. Can you believe he's actually had the gall to use me as his alibi?"

"And is he telling the truth? Can you vouch for him?"

"I'm afraid I can." He squirmed in the passenger seat. "I have no choice. He's supposed to have killed someone at the time he was at my mum's funeral — so there we have it. His alibi stands up,"

"Not good, Tom. Well, not for your promotion prospects anyway."

"Too damn true it isn't. I do nothing wrong, but still my career suffers from setback after setback. This shouldn't make it any worse but it sure as hell won't do it any good either. Anyway, what's your excuse? You're looking almost as bad as me." There were dark circles under Ruth's eyes.

"At least I wasn't late this morning."

"Even so, you're hardly at your best, are you? So come on — tell me what's really going on."

"I was out with Jake last night. We got talking, well arguing mostly. We seem to want different things. Well, to be honest, I don't really know what I want." She let out a long sigh. "Sometimes I wish I was like other women. Everyone I know who's my age is married with kids. Why don't I want that, sir?"

"It's the job. It gets to you, takes over your entire life, and there's not a damn thing you can do about it. But you know that. So you've got a decision to make. You like him, and that causes problems — inside here." He tapped his head.

"So says the expert. And you? Any luck with Monika?"

"I've not tried. I can't see why she'd want anything to do with me after . . . Well, after Lydia."

Ruth laughed and shook her head. "The image of you standing there, shame-faced, waiting for a lift that morning, after you'd spent the night with the blonde bimbo, was priceless. But even so, I still think you should try. Lydia's out of the way now, and you and Monika were good together."

"I don't think *good together* is quite enough, Ruth."

"But isn't it worth another go? I'm sure Monika would be up for that. She misses you. I know her, remember, and I can tell. If you like, I can put in a word for you."

"No, it's okay. I can do my own grovelling, thank you very much."

"Well make sure you grovel nicely. You saw her at the funeral. Didn't you notice how she's lost weight, grown her hair and styled it differently?"

Truthfully, he hadn't — idiot! So she'd been hoping to impress him and he hadn't even spotted the difference. What did that say about where his head was?

"Well, at least you've got your Zoe for company now, haven't you?"

"Yep, and it's good having her around." He smiled. "Do you think she's happy here? Has she said anything to you?"

Ruth shrugged. "We haven't really had time to get to know each other that well. But she always seems okay. She's got herself a good job. It's a start."

But was it enough? Calladine wanted his daughter to be happy. He wanted her to stay in his life. He was acutely aware that the job got in the way of that relationship too. He was always busy, always going somewhere. But if Zoe suddenly decided to up sticks and return to Bristol, he'd be devastated.

Zoe, Monika . . . he really had to sort out what to do about the women in his life. If he just let things slide — as he usually did — then he could end up completely alone again, and he didn't want that, not anymore.

They pulled into the hospital car park.

"If you like, I'll go and talk to Stone and you can see if Doc Hoyle has the PM report for us yet."

Alexander Stone was sitting up in bed reading a newspaper. He looked a great deal better than yesterday; his face wasn't so red and inflamed.

"DI Calladine, Leesworth Police. We met briefly when you were brought in. I don't know how much you know about what happened yesterday, but a woman's body was found in the back of your car." He saw the look of horror cross the man's face. "We know now it wasn't you who put her there, so don't worry; I'm not about to arrest you or anything. I simply want to know what you recall, what you saw. Do you remember seeing anyone else?"

"Not really, it's all a bit of a haze. It seemed like a bloody nightmare at the time. I was frantic with pain, and then when he turned up and poured petrol everywhere, I just kept shouting for him to stop, and when he flicked that match I went completely to pieces. To be honest I didn't know what he was doing. I didn't even see the woman."

"You were very lucky. Things could have been much worse. A combination of heavy rain and the fire crew saved your bacon. Did you get a look at him, the bloke who did this?"

"No. I couldn't move. I couldn't even turn my head, but I saw his van. It was small and white. Being white it showed up, even through the fog."

Very useful. How many small white vans, he wondered, were registered in Leesworth — if that's where their man came from? "What time was this, Mr Stone?"

"I'd been travelling since six, so it must have been about seven thirty; certainly no later."

Calladine's mobile rang. It was Ruth. He nodded an apology to Stone and walked a few feet away to answer it.

"Sir, I'm with the doc. He wants to talk to you as well, so I'll wait for you here."

What now? The PM must have thrown up something controversial. Calladine told Stone that a detective would be along to take his statement later, and left him in peace.

* * *

"Doesn't make pleasant reading, Tom." Calladine could see from the pathologist's face that this one had affected him. The way the body looked; the dreadful possibilities — fair enough, it had got to him too.

"She was murdered. Garrotted. It's all in there." The doctor spoke wearily. "You should know that she was pregnant too, only a few weeks along. The blood on her legs was from a botched abortion attempt. From the state of the uterus I'd say something sharp was used vaginally."

Calladine felt his stomach heave. Poor girl. "It's bad then."

"The worst. And the body had been moved very recently, as you thought. There are marks on her feet, particularly her heels where she was probably dragged across the road, possibly from one vehicle to the other. Julian has taken samples of the grit found in the wounds and will compare it with that found on the bypass."

Pregnant. And he'd tried to abort it. Doc's description of what had happened to the girl made Calladine think of a medieval torture chamber.

"Julian's also analysing the rust samples taken from her wrists and ankles. It might throw up something. I found fine metal slivers in the wound on her neck, so she was garrotted with a wire. She wasn't anorexic either: she was starved. Her stomach had shrunk and her muscles show evidence of wasting."

"Was there anything about the body that might help us identify her?" Ruth asked. "What about the DNA?"

"There's no match on the database, I'm afraid, and no fingerprint match either. But the good news is she had an orthopaedic plate fitted in her wrist."

"What d'you mean?"

"At some time in the past — within the last three years, at a guess, extrapolating from the bone development — she'd had a nasty fracture to her wrist. The bones had to be plated together to help them heal. The plate remains in situ; they are very rarely removed. The fixation plate from her wrist has numbers on it — batch numbers. With a lot of research and some luck you may be able to use it to trace her. Details are in the report."

"So what do we do now?"

"We go back to the station and make a start, that's what." Calladine flicked through the report quickly. "Thanks, Doc. Keep me posted on anything else you get."

Chapter 8

"I know we're short-handed, but we've got a lot on. We've several research tasks that need doing urgently. With regards to the murdered girl, it looks like the only way forward at the moment," Calladine told his team. "Imogen and Rocco drew a blank at the nursery. All of Alton's delivery notes checked out, so it looks like he's in the clear. Check Cassie Rigby's birth details. Make it a priority. The kid's been missing for over twenty-four hours now. If we don't find something very soon I'll have to call time and pass it on." He sighed. That would be grim — the prospect of an abducted child, possibly worse. He paused for a moment. The team were lively enough, raring to go in fact. But, like him, they needed progress, and at present they were going around in circles.

"The big job on the murder case is tracing the plate found in the girl's arm. It could have come from anywhere, any country. But we might start with the NHS first. Imogen — I know you're on the Rigby case right now, but see what you can do."

He knew Imogen was good at ferreting out information that the others seemed to miss, particularly where using the internet was concerned.

"Yes, sir. I'll do the Rigby checks first though. We need to find the kid."

She was right. That had to come first. There was a lot to do, and they were spread very thin. Could DCI Jones offer anything, he wondered? He'd go and discuss it with him when they'd finished here.

"Okay. We'd better get on. Get to it this afternoon and we'll resume tomorrow."

He picked up the report on what they'd found so far about the murdered girl, and went to find Jones. The man was a shambles. Calladine doubted he had any idea about what really went on at the station, and how short of people they were.

"Sir!" The DCI was about to lock his office door. Alright for some. He'd appreciate an early dart himself sometimes.

"We're a little stretched, sir. I was hoping to discuss it with you."

"I've got an appointment, Tom. Can it wait until tomorrow?"

"I suppose it'll have to. But can I ask you to have a look at this? Perhaps tonight?"

DCI Jones frowned but took the folder.

* * *

"I know there's no record of the Rigbys having a child," Imogen told Rocco. But I've drawn a blank under Mrs Rigby's maiden name too.'

"So what's going on? She didn't spring out of thin air. Someone gave birth to her," Rocco replied.

"Indeed. But that someone wasn't Jane Rigby, so it would seem. I think we should go back and talk to them again. Push them a bit like the boss suggested."

"Okay. We can go now if you want." At last Rocco was getting back into it; beginning to enjoy the cut and thrust of an investigation. Right now, the icing on the cake would be finding the child.

60

The Rigbys lived in a neat semi on the outskirts of Leesdon. Rocco rang the doorbell and PC Kate Robinson answered.

"She's having a rest. But he's here," she said.

PC Robinson led the way into the sitting room, where Robert Rigby was seated, staring out into the gloom of his winter-worn garden.

"Bad time of year. Hate it when nothing grows." He smiled. "Have you found Cassie yet?"

"No, Mr Rigby, and we're going to have to ask you some more questions, I'm afraid."

"I don't see why. I doubt I can add anything. I wasn't there, so I can't imagine what you think I can offer."

"Well, you can tell me where Cassie was born for a start."

"Well, in the General, down the road." Rigby appeared to be completely unfazed by the question.

"No she wasn't, Mr Rigby. Well if she was, not to you and your wife anyway."

He fell silent and studied his hands for a moment or two. "I'm afraid you have me there, Detective Constable."

Just as Imogen was about to ask him what he meant by that, there was a noise from the hallway. Mrs Rigby was coming down the stairs to join them.

"But I don't see that that matters. Cassie is still missing, and you still need to find her."

Jane Rigby came into the room. "Tell them, Robert. They'll find out in time anyway." She looked a mess. Her hair was dishevelled and her face was tired and drawn. Robert Rigby remained stubbornly silent.

Realising her husband wasn't going to talk, she cast him a doleful look, and began to speak. "She's adopted — well, fostered really. Isn't that right, Robert?"

He remained silent, his eyes never leaving the window.

"But long-term, we want to keep her. We've had Cassie since she was a baby and she's content with us. We can give her everything; make her happy. That drug-sodden mother of hers couldn't do anything for her. Tell me, Constable — if you were Cassie, who would you choose to live with?"

Jane Rigby sat on the sofa beside her husband and made to hold his hand, but he moved away. She continued:

"We couldn't have children of our own. Being able to foster was a godsend, and Cassie was a beautiful baby. We both fell in love with her, didn't we, Robert? She had blonde hair and big blue eyes, and her natural mother was far too young and wild to cope. We had hoped that we'd be able to adopt, you know, in time, but her natural mother wouldn't give permission. I can't understand why she should have any say in the matter. She's never bothered with Cassie until recently."

Robert Rigby cleared his throat. What was going on inside his head? Imogen wondered. What was it he wasn't saying?

"Did you want to keep her, Mr Rigby?"

"Of course he did. How can you ask such a question? Robert loved little Cassie — does love little Cassie . . ." She dissolved in a fresh flood of tears.

"Did her natural mother want her back?"

"Well she can't have her back," Jane Rigby snapped. "She's not suitable. She's a mess and it'd never be allowed."

"Does Cassie know her?"

Jane Rigby nodded. "Yes, she does now. She's seen both her mother and her maternal grandmother recently. Like I said, during the past few months they've come and visited from time to time." She looked at her husband, her eyes wild with fear. "You think they've taken her. You do, don't you? That's why you won't say anything, isn't it, Robert? Something's isn't right — it's the way we got Cassie in the first place — isn't it?"

Imogen's eyes went from one to the other.

"What was wrong with the way you got Cassie, Mrs Rigby?"

"Nothing . . . I'm not sure." She nudged her husband, but he shrugged her away. "We never saw Social Services for a start. Don't you think that odd?"

Yes it was. It was becoming clear that Cassie hadn't been fostered at all — not in the accepted sense. But what was the arrangement between the Rigbys and the child's natural mother?

"Do you think Cassie would go off with her mother?" It would certainly explain why the child had disappeared so quietly. If a stranger had approached and tried to take hold of her, the chances were that she'd have screamed blue murder.

Jane Rigby nodded, and buried her face in a hanky again. Her husband remained silent.

"I want her name and address." There was no answer. "Mrs Rigby, Mr Rigby, if we are to find Cassie, then you are going to have to help us. If you won't, then I'll get the details I need from Social Services."

Robert Rigby looked up. Imogen could tell from the look he gave her that his wife had been telling the truth — Social Services had never been part of the bargain. The frightened expression on his face said it all.

Jane Rigby took a pen and notepad from the coffee table, and scribbled down an address. "Now please go. I don't want you here. I just want Cassie back. You have to find her!"

* * *

"So why not just tell us all that in the first place?" Rocco asked, once the detectives were outside. "Sometimes I just don't understand people. Why all the obstacles? What is it they're afraid of?"

"Us — the law, you idiot. They shouldn't legally have had Cassie in the first place. I bet they've made some arrangement with her natural mother, and now one side has reneged on the deal."

"You think the Rigbys bought the kid?"

"I don't know. We'll find Cassie first and deal with that bit later."

"He did look shit-scared when Social Services were mentioned."

Imogen looked at the details Jane Rigby had given her. "With a bit of luck we could have this wound up before close of play." But when she read the address, she frowned. "She lives on the Hobfield, Rocco. Are you sure you're up to this?"

Up to it or not, he had little choice. This was his job, and the young DC had no intention of giving it up any time soon.

"Where?"

"Heron Tower. Isn't that where . . . ?"

"Where I got clobbered? Yes it is. But I've got to move on, and I don't want to be mollycoddled. So it's fine. We'll just do our job, okay?" Rocco buttoned his overcoat and turned the collar up. What was the use? It was bound to happen one day. Things being what they were around here, he couldn't avoid the Hobfield forever.

* * *

The curtains were pulled tight shut. Rocco banged on the door of the flat and called her name, but there was no reply. Imogen put her face to the glass and could just make out a shadow flitting past. She was in there.

"Janine! I've seen you. I know you're there." She banged on the door again. Several minutes passed, and finally the young woman came to the door.

"Miss Felton? DC Goode and DC Rockliffe from Leesworth CID. Can we come in and ask you a few questions, please?"

Janine Felton didn't reply. She led the way in silence into a small sitting room. The place was untidy —

downright dirty in fact, and Imogen wrinkled her nose at the smell. The place was a sharp contrast to the Rigbys' home.

"The dog. How am I expected to take him out when I live on the seventh floor?"

"Do you know where Cassandra is, Miss Felton?" Rocco was growing impatient.

"Course I do. What sort of parent d'you think I am?"

He didn't really want to answer that.

"She's with my mother in Scarborough." She lifted a phone off the table and keyed in a number. "Here — ask her yourself. You don't have to take my word for it."

She handed Imogen the phone as a woman answered.

"Are you Janine Felton's mother?" Imogen exchanged a few words with the person on the other end of the line, and then nodded and handed the phone back. "Thank you, Janine. You have no right to take Cassie like that. You could at least have said something to the Rigbys. They have been out of their minds with worry. I presume it was you who took Cassie from the café? You do realise that it could be classed as kidnap?"

"They've sent you, haven't they? No — it's her. She's the one sent you. Stupid bitch knows nothing about our little arrangement because he was too bloody scared to tell her."

"Too scared to tell her what, Janine?"

"About our little arrangement. He stopped paying, so I took Cassie back. It's that simple. No crime's been committed, so I don't know what you lot are involved for. It's down to him. All he has to do is make the payments as arranged, and I'll leave well enough alone."

"Are you telling us that Mr and Mrs Rigby were paying you for Cassie?"

"Too bloody right I am. What use is a kid to me? This is no place for anyone, never mind a child."

Imogen looked gobsmacked. She shook her head and glanced at Rocco, groping for a way forward.

"I didn't do anything wrong. My mother wanted her. When he didn't make this month's payment, she insisted I get her back. And they did know, the Rigbys — well he did. So don't look at me like that. She's my child, for fuck's sake, so get off my case. Anyway, they were supposed to be handing her back for a couple of days before Christmas, so what difference does it make?"

"So why is Cassie with your mother now?"

"I just told you, stupid! Because we're both going to stay there for Christmas — get away from this hell hole."

"So Social Services know nothing about this? Cassie is not officially fostered with the Rigbys?"

"No, she damn well isn't, and isn't likely to be if I have anything to do with it."

Janine Felton lit a cigarette and swore under her breath.

"My mum wants to keep her. It's nice where she is, by the sea. Cassie is fond of her." Janine handed Imogen a scrap of paper with an address on it. "I have no problem with Cassie being with my mum — so that's that. Not a bloody thing you can do about it."

Imogen rang the station. A quick conversation with Joyce, and the Scarborough police would give the grandmother a visit. So that was it: an argument about custody. Imogen decided they should return to the station and confirm what Janine had told them. She'd tell Social Services too. But what to do about the Rigbys? Perhaps that'd be better left for the experts to sort out.

"Resolved," Rocco announced with a shake of his head. "I'm going to ring the boss and tell him the kid's safe — it'll make his day. Then can we get out of here, please? I hate this place."

Imogen would ring WPC Kate Robinson and get her to pass the news to the Rigbys. That was going to be a tricky conversation. Imogen knew she couldn't promise them anything. Robert Rigby had paid for a child. He'd lied to his wife and Social Services had been kept completely out of the loop. There would be repercussions, she felt sure.

* * *

"Sir, we've found Cassie Rigby. She's in Scarborough with her maternal grandmother and quite safe. So no harm done."

Calladine had dozed off on his sofa and woke with a start when his mobile rang. The news was good, very good, the best in fact. The last thing he wanted was the Cassie Rigby thing to drag on, or become something worse. Now they could put all their efforts into finding whoever had murdered that girl.

He rubbed his head and winced — it ached. He was beginning to wonder how long he could keep this up — the late nights, no proper sleep and the stress. He looked around; there was no sign of Zoe either. Another night away from home. What was going on? Had she met someone?

He was about to phone her when his mobile rang again. This time it was Doc Hoyle.

"Sorry to ring you at home, Tom. But it is important. We've got another nasty one. The body of a young woman was left in the back of a hearse at the undertakers this evening."

Just what he needed. The sound of those words echoed through his aching head, making his stomach churn.

"Okay, I'll come down. Are there any similarities with the murder of the other girl?"

"Early days, but yes, I'd say so. There was the same sort of stuff with the teeth. But you should know — this one's been dead a lot longer. She's quite badly decomposed."

Was their man running scared? Why dump the body now? And where the hell had she been kept? He rubbed his aching head again. "The undertakers in Leesdon, you said?"

"Yes. There was no coffin in the hearse at the time, so she was simply slid in, wrapped in a blanket."

"Give me twenty minutes and I'll be with you."

* * *

Calladine decided this was one he could do on his own — Ruth needed the downtime. There wasn't really much to see anyway. The back of the hearse was open and Doc Hoyle was leaning inside.

"She's been wrapped in a blanket and for some time, I'd say. The smell is bad. It's my guess she was buried and then dug up a few days ago. She's been kept somewhere reasonably warm — there are maggots."

"There's a camera up there." Calladine nodded, pointing the thing out for Julian, who'd joined them.

"I'll get on it, Inspector." Julian wrinkled his nose at the smell of decomposition. "I'll have the vehicle checked — fingerprints, soil and shoe tracks left on the path — the lot."

"For now we'll take the photos of the body as we found it and I'll start the PM at eight in the morning," the doctor decided. "It won't be pretty, Tom — just warning you."

* * *

On his return home, Calladine rang Ruth and arranged to meet her at the mortuary early the next morning. He could hear music in the background and a male voice talking — Jake Ireson he presumed. He'd been right not to have her come with him. Hopefully she was making progress. He'd had every intention of speaking to Monika earlier but had fallen asleep instead, and now this. He no longer had the energy. Damping down the fire, he put his empty whiskey glass in the kitchen sink, and went to bed.

＊ ＊ ＊

But Ruth and Jake hadn't been talking — they'd been arguing. It had started innocently enough with a simple question – did she want to go visit his parents at the weekend? Ruth's stomach had flipped — she was going to have to disappoint him yet again. Jake's parents lived in Whitby.

"We've a lot on — two murders and a missing child case to clear up." She shook her head.

"So when do I get a look in? If you're not working, then you're messing about with that birdwatching group of yours. He rang earlier, Reg thingy."

"Reg Hope, and wind your neck in. If I didn't know better I'd say you were jealous. Reg is sixty-two and retired. He's a friend; he takes photographs of birds and sticks them on his blog. He's great fun and I like him. So get off my back!"

"And me? Do you think I'm great fun?"

She turned to look at him. What did she think? Fun? Definitely not, of late. But she did like him, and that was the problem.

"When things get slacker — which they will," she reassured him, "we'll go and see your parents. It won't be long. Just let us get this case wrapped up."

He was sat in his shirt sleeves by the fire, marking exercise books. He shook his head and tutted.

"Are you growing a beard?" She tried to change the subject.

"It's for the play. The sixth form are putting on *Macbeth*, and they want me in it."

"You love it, don't you?" Ruth said, punching his arm playfully. "I bet all those teenage girls have a right crush on the dishy Mr Ireson."

"I know what you're trying to do, and it won't work. We need to spend more time together, or this relationship is doomed. You said so yourself; even your boss has history."

"This has nothing to do with Tom, it's all me. You have to understand, Jake, I am my job. It's my life. It's what I do." She was on the verge of tears. He had to understand. She was not about to give it up, not even for him. She still had ambition: Ruth wanted to make inspector before she reached forty.

"So you rule out everything else, even me?" He stood up. "Well I'm sick of it, Ruth. I don't think this relationship is going anywhere, and I'm in no mood to piss about. I thought we had something. You thought that too, at one time. So what happened?"

"Nothing, Jake, nothing happened. It's just my job."

At that moment the phone rang, and casting an apologetic glance his way, Ruth answered it.

From the tone of her voice, and what she was saying, Jake knew it was Calladine. He grabbed his books and stormed off upstairs to the study.

Chapter 9

Day Four

As he met Ruth at the mortuary door, Calladine apologised. "Hope I didn't interrupt anything last night. I heard Jake's voice in the background. Did it go well?"

"Sort of, but I still can't decide what to do about my love life."

"You and me both." He tried to joke, but the truth was, the Monika problem wasn't funny — not in the least. What with her and the case, his mind was constantly active. He'd tossed and turned most of the night, and the repercussions were making themselves felt.

"You need to get it fixed, Tom. It's all very well giving me advice, but you need to take a good long look at your own life. You're weary. It shows on your face. It's all taking its toll. If you're not careful the job will get the better of you, and then where will we all be?"

Tom Calladine was well aware he'd looked better. His features were drawn and there was a slight ashen tone to his face that was made worse by his progressively greying hair. He was looking his age and feeling the strain.

"Not sleeping is a pain in the arse. But I expect it'll pass. In the meantime, we must get on. We can't let up on this. Make a decision, Ruth — only then will things settle down in here." He tapped his head. "You give it a go and I'll join you. Let's see what we can achieve by the end of the week."

"I'd love to, but I've got the most awful feeling I've dithered about for too long — that I've put him off once too often. You know how it is — you spend so much time pleasing yourself, it's hard to make changes. And having someone permanent in your life certainly changes things."

"Permanent — that's a big word. Personally I think it's about time you found yourself a good man. It's worth giving it a go, surely? It's good to have someone to go home to at the end of the day. Zoe's made a huge difference."

"That's different, guv. Zoe's your daughter. Where Jake's concerned I'll have to see — and you're a fine one to talk anyway. If it's about time for me to settle down, then what about you? You skip from one woman to the next like a randy teenager! And I bet you haven't spoken to Monika yet — have you?" She watched him frown. "Coward. You're afraid she'll lay into you for what you did."

"It's not that. To be honest it'd be a relief if she did. If she gave me a right bollocking, then I might feel better. It's the injured looks and accusing stares I can't stand."

"Still . . . I'd think about it if I were you. But for the time being we've got our hands full with this little lot." Ruth pushed on the mortuary door.

"Randy teenager. So that's what you think of me. I wish I was; they don't know what they've got — none of them do."

"This is going to be bad, isn't it? I mean it must be if she's been in the ground for a while." Ruth paused for a moment with her hand still on the door handle.

Calladine nodded. "We've done this before, haven't we? So try and stay detached."

"What I'm trying to get my head around with all this, is why no one's been reported missing. I had a quick look at the *mispers* list and no one comes close. I have to ask myself why that is. Do we have to cast our net much, much wider? Could we even be looking at illegals here?"

That wasn't a bad idea. But if they were, then they'd never get anywhere, because no one would talk.

"Tracing that plate will help — that is if we get anywhere with it. There are thousands and thousands of those damn things fitted every year. Anyway, the good news is that Cassie Rigby is safe," Calladine said. "Imogen and Rocco got that little mystery solved last night. It was good work, and it looks like Rocco is well and truly back on board now. The Rigbys will have to be sorted, though. Buying a child can't be tolerated. I can't say what the outcome will be, but it's doubtful they'll have any further contact with Cassie."

* * *

Both detectives made their way to a gallery above the table where the young woman's body was laid out. Doc Hoyle, his assistant and Julian were getting things ready below. Doc Hoyle looked up and smiled, fixed his mask over his face and pulled on his gloves. His assistant pulled back the sheet to reveal the girl.

Neither Calladine nor Ruth was prepared for the sight. The girl's body looked almost black with decay. Most of her abdomen and her chest cavity had rotted away, leaving a rather gruesome arrangement of ribs that supported remnants of skin. Her head was practically a skull, the facial features indistinguishable. Doc Hoyle hadn't exaggerated when he'd said she'd been dead a lot longer than the first girl. Even from this distance the smell was bad and they willingly picked up the masks left out for them.

The pathologist began, "Female, and she's been dead and buried in what looks like soil for a while. She was buried naked, wrapped in the blanket we found her in. It's badly stained and sticking to the body." He began gently peeling it away, removing some of the dirt from what was left of her limbs with a fine brush. "I'll have a sample of the soil tested. It might tell us something." He put some into a container and handed it to Julian.

The pathologist looked up at the two detectives and shook his head. "I'd say she was killed during the last few months. Time of death is nigh impossible to determine. It's been cold and that hinders decomposition. The body will yield some information, but the tests will take time. Julian will crack on but you'll have to give us a day or two at least. One thing I'm fairly confident about — she's from the same stable as the last one." He tweezered up a small metallic object from the blanket beside her skull, dropping it into a kidney dish. "Another livestock tag. Looking at it quickly I'd say this one says *Vida 3*."

What was it with that damn word? Name? Place? He needed to know. It was looking highly likely now that it was a name. Calladine couldn't think of any other rational explanation — not that anything about this seemed at all rational.

Doc Hoyle carefully examined what little was left of her face. "Her teeth have been mutilated and, although the state of the body makes it difficult, I'd say she was garrotted like the other one. Her trachea is split in two." He indicated for the assistant to take a photo. "She was slight and there are still clumps of long, fair hair left on the remaining scalp tissue. Her abdomen is interesting . . ." The doctor concentrated for a moment. "It is probable that this girl was pregnant too." The loud tick of the mortuary clock filled the silence. All eyes were on the pathologist. Ruth jumped slightly as something was dropped into a stainless steel kidney dish.

"Further checks will confirm, but I'm almost sure the piece of bone is from a foetus. Given the size of it she would have to have been twenty weeks or more. I'll do a DNA test to make sure and compare it to the foetus from the other girl — ascertain whether it's the same father."

* * *

Ruth felt sick. The room was swimming and had suddenly become very claustrophobic. There could be no mistake. They had another one. Was that why he got rid of them? Because they got pregnant? She didn't dare think about what had happened to the poor girl, and what she must have gone through. But whatever it was, it must have been every bit as bad as with *Vida 5*.

She had to pull herself together. There was a job to do. It was warm in here and, despite the mask, the smell was getting to her and making her feel faint. She thought for a moment that she'd been staring at the table for too long because she could swear something around the body was moving. The room seemed to sway again and she grabbed Calladine's arm to steady herself. She blinked a couple of times and shook her head. Finally she gasped, still clinging to Calladine's arm, "Did you see that?"

The doctor looked up. "Wildlife, Ruth. All sorts of creepy crawlies have taken up residence in the body. Not to mention a good few maggots . . . I'm going to have to clean her up a bit. The maggots might tell us something." Julian handed him a small container and he plopped some into it. "This will take time. I can't risk spoiling anything that might be helpful."

Maggots! He wasn't joking either. The more looked, the more she saw.

"There are bite marks on her arms — predation, I'd say, and her right foot is missing. If I had to make an educated guess, from the marks, I'd say the work of a fox."

"I'll have to leave, sir. I can't stand to listen to any more."

75

The idea of that poor girl ending up as nothing more than a meal for the foxes was making her heave.

Ruth Bayliss ran from the room and stood outside Doc Hoyle's office, leaning against the wall and breathing deeply. That was one of the most horrific sights she'd ever seen, and she'd seen a fair few by now.

They had a bloody nutter on the loose. This was a maniac who took young women and killed them in the most horrendous ways. He had to be stopped. Everything else would have to be put on hold until they did — and that included Jake Ireson.

He wouldn't like it. There was no way she would be able to visit his parents in Whitby this weekend. It was going to be like this always. She could see argument after argument looming in front of her, as Jake got tired of her excuses. She closed her eyes. Why had Jake's parents decided to retire to Whitby? Why couldn't they have moved into a bungalow in Leesdon instead?

"Sorry, Ruth." The doctor and Calladine were coming towards her. "She's been somewhere above ground for a day or two — hence the maggots, the smell and the accelerated decomposition. Somewhere relatively warm I'd say, so the flies and the animals have got to her. The beetles and the worms were picked up underground, but not the maggots. The damage is fairly new too, and not from when she was first killed," Hoyle said.

Ruth wondered how he could be so matter of fact about it all. A good thing, too. Someone had to gather the evidence.

* * *

He was meeting her for lunch — her idea. She'd taken the bait with hardly any effort on his part at all. She'd enjoyed herself so much on Tuesday night she wanted more. She said it was a change to have someone who could afford the good things in life. He wasn't taken in. She liked his money, and that was the real reason she was so keen to see him again. It was pointless going out with another student, she'd told him. They were always broke.

For now he was happy to indulge her. It smoothed the way for the next part of his plan. So he would have to spend a few pounds — so what? All that would end soon enough. Then she'd learn the hard facts. She'd learn what it was really like to be Vida. Now there was a woman; a proper lady. She hadn't been interested in his money — she'd had plenty of her own.

But meeting Patsy Lumis again meant shelving work for the day, and that was a real pain. He'd have to explain himself — make some excuse and grovel. He hated that; it was demeaning, and he hated his job — he hated being taken for granted.

He'd spend the morning preparing. There was a lot to do. His special place had to be perfect for its next inhabitant. Still, women like her were hard to find, so, in the end, it would be worth it. He'd clean up a bit, make it smell sweet, and clean his instruments. The thought of wielding all that stainless steel once again, with purpose, made him excited. He could feel that special thrill. He flexed his fingers.

Dentistry was difficult to learn, but he had to master it. How else was he going to impress Vida? It was a skill she greatly admired. She'd spoken a lot about her own dentist, about the work she'd had done. He wanted to be good at it too, so he could keep things as she wanted them. A smile like Vida's took a great deal of maintenance, and he'd hoped to be a lot better at it by now but there were always unforeseen difficulties. With the first one he'd not thought it through; he'd not thought about the blood or the saliva and so he'd botched it completely.

They fought too and screamed. But he got around that by strapping them down. He cut out all the crying and pleading by stitching their swollen, ugly mouths tight shut. He didn't do it nicely, either — no painkillers. He'd quickly realised that he enjoyed watching them suffer. He derived a whole heap of pleasure from putting them through it. To that end he always used thick string or garden twine — the kind with wire running through it — to seal those soft, fleshy lips that always bled so much and swelled so hideously. The thought made him chuckle.

He couldn't rationalise it to himself. On the one hand he loved the sound of those American accents, so much like Vida's. On the other, he hated the recriminations, the name calling; the violent language they all spouted. And, of course, he knew very well that none of them was really Vida, and that always made him angry, because he tried really hard. He fixed their hair and makeup, provided the right clothing, and of course, the perfect teeth to match Vida's lovely smile. But he never quite pulled it off. When he grew angry he assuaged it by treating them cruelly. He preferred the mouths to be silent. They were far easier to deal with — particularly afterwards, when he could use their bodies for his sexual pleasure.

He closed his eyes. Yes, he was wicked, truly wicked, and he needed saving from himself. Vida could save him. If she'd agree to be his, then all this would end and he'd be happy. But the bitch would have nothing to do with him. That made him angry. It made him want to do those dreadful things to the girls. It was all her fault.

They'd agreed to meet in Manchester again. She wanted to go to a restaurant in Chinatown for lunch. He dressed a little more casually this time: smart pants and a good shirt. He topped it all off with his leather jacket, and set out to catch the train.

She was waiting for him in St. Peter's Square. She ran to his side and kissed his cheek. A little keen for so soon in the relationship, but who was he to complain? He liked it.

She talked non-stop; a load of rubbish. She complained about the course she was on, her tutors, and the crappy accommodation she had to live in. Jack tried to be sympathetic. He made all the right noises, but sympathy just wasn't his style. In an effort to shut her up, he held her hand and pointed to the restaurant he was taking her to. It would be easy to silence her once he got her to his place.

The restaurant was an upmarket, rather expensive eatery that was sure to impress. He knew her weakness now. It was obvious because she made no secret of it. She was a gold digger. So — Jack would promise her the jackpot.

"Jack, you're so good to me!" She took his arm and pulled him along the road towards the entrance. "I'm so hungry. Can we have like one of those banquet things? You don't know what it's like being a poor ol' student." She batted long dark lashes at him. "My Mom says I've got to manage. She says if I can't, then I'll just have to come back home." She pouted. "You don't want me to have to do that — do you, Jack?"

No, he damn well didn't. He'd done all the planning and preparation for her. This one wasn't going anywhere.

"If I had a man who really liked me, who'd look after me, then I'm sure I'd stay."

"In that case I'll just have to take good care of you." He put his arm around her waist as they walked. She was an open book; shallow and grasping — well, she'd pay the price for that soon enough. "You can come to mine. Have a bit of a break — tomorrow night." He bent down to kiss her cheek. "I'll pick you up. Pack a few things. I've got plenty of room. I'll send out for some food. We can eat and drink and have a good time getting to know each other."

Chapter 10

"Here." With a flourish, Julian Batho handed Imogen a piece of paper. "The firm that manufactured the orthopaedic plate is called 'Partridges of Birmingham'."

Imogen Goode was sat at her desk poring over some paperwork. "You looked it up?" She hardly dared to believe her luck. "And you actually found it? How did you do it?"

The forensic scientist played nervously with his glasses and gave her a dismissive shrug. He wouldn't admit it, but he'd really slogged to find the information for her. He liked her; he liked her a lot. All he needed now was the courage to tell her and then ask her out. And that was the problem. Forensic science was one thing, but asking an attractive woman for a night out was beyond him. She was so perfect, so pretty, so completely the opposite of him. Tall and clever he might be, but he was no looker. It leeched at his confidence.

"It was a little easier for me. I know who the main manufacturers are in this country so I tried them first. The number you're looking for is in that batch there." He pointed to the paper. "If you ring them they should be able to tell you which hospital they went to."

"I owe you, Julian. DI Calladine will be pleased too. We need this, we really do. We've got another one this morning. The DI and Ruth are with Doc Hoyle now."

"I know. I was there earlier, helping the doctor. I've got a whole lot of samples to work on, so I'd better get back to the lab. I've got to go to the undertakers. The hearse she was found in needs going over with a fine toothcomb. I'll be in touch if I get anything else." He smiled at her.

"When this is sorted I'll take you out for a slap-up dinner," she promised. "Don't let me forget!"

No he wouldn't. It was a start. When the time came he'd make sure he had a raft of suggestions ready so she didn't try to wheedle out of keeping her side of the bargain.

* * *

Imogen rang the manufacturer right away, and found out that the plate had gone to a local hospital.

"I've found it, sir!" She practically shouted down the phone to Calladine. "Well, I had a little help from Julian, but we've got the info on the orthopaedic plate."

That was the best piece of news Calladine had heard all week — apart from finding Cassie Rigby.

"You'll never believe it but she was treated locally too — at the Infirmary in Central Manchester. I've rung them, and the records people are digging out the details as we speak."

"Great work, Imogen. Thank Julian for me too. Did the records people say how long?"

"They are going to courier them across to us — should be anytime soon. I'll bell you when we get them."

"Ruth and I are still at the mortuary. When you get a name let me know and we'll go into town and talk to whoever treated her."

Ruth was sipping tea — hot, sweet tea — trying to get her head back together after the nightmare of the PM room.

"I wish I wasn't such a wimp. But it gets to me, Tom. That poor girl — what she must have suffered! Her, and the other one too. What is this nutter doing? What are his reasons — if he has any, that is?"

"People who do these things have their own rationale for their behaviour. Inside his twisted mind it'll make perfect sense. It's just the rest of us that are left guessing."

"There are more out there, aren't there? It's the numbers. We've got number five and now three, so there's bound to be more. I'm right, aren't I?"

Calladine nodded. Somewhere out there were numbers one, two and four. Knowing that made him edgy. He had questions he couldn't answer, such as had this bastard taken anyone after Vida 5? Did he, even now, have his latest victim imprisoned somewhere? Was he torturing some other girl to death? Where did he find them? And how come they were all so anonymous? These questions and more swirled around in his head. He needed to make sense of everything they'd got up to now. He needed to get back to the nick.

"The good news is we've got a lead on the plate. Imogen is going to ring back, and with a bit of luck we'll get a name. Then we really will have something to go on."

* * *

The something was a student called Madison Benneti. The hospital confirmed that they'd fitted the orthopaedic plate just over three years ago, and that she'd been a student at the university in Manchester. She'd given her address at that time as the halls of residence, so the university was their next call.

"The person you need to see is a Mrs Johnson," a receptionist told them. "She was Madison's course tutor and she'll know what happened to her."

Wishful thinking. Joanna Johnson had no idea what had become of Madison Benneti, nor did she seem to care.

"One day she's here, doing fine, the next she's gone. Students can be like that sometimes. They get a place here, then they find they don't like the course. Studying wasn't really Madison's thing; that was pretty obvious from her grades. I'm afraid she had an agenda of her own. Madison made no secret of the fact that she'd come to the UK specifically to look for a husband — a rich one. Rumour had it that she'd finally met him. Who he was, I couldn't tell you, but that was always her plan from the off."

"Came to the UK from where?" Ruth asked.

"From the USA. New York, I believe."

So definitely not local, then.

"We're going to need a proper address. We need to contact her family urgently," Calladine told her.

"From what I remember, Madison didn't get on with her parents. Look — I don't know why you're here, but take my word for it, Madison Benneti is probably married to her Mr Perfect by now, and living in the lap of luxury."

"Madison is dead, Mrs Johnson. She was murdered. So I think you should give us that address, because they need to be told, don't you think?"

Calladine couldn't believe the woman's attitude. Wasn't she supposed to look out for the students under her watch? So then how come one of them had been allowed to simply disappear?

"I didn't realise. You should have said straight away. You have to understand, I look after dozens of students, and I can't be on top of them all. Come with me and I'll get you the information."

She led the way down a flight of stairs and into a small office. "I'll get her details from the system — just give me a minute."

She tapped away at the keyboard and sent a document to the printer. "Madison left in such a hurry — of course I asked around, but no one could volunteer anything useful.

With her ambitions in the husband department, what was I supposed to do?"

"Didn't you think to contact the authorities — the American Embassy or the immigration people?"

"Well no. Madison wasn't an isolated case. Each year we lose a small number of foreign students. It's just the way it is, I'm afraid. Resources dictate what can be done about it, Inspector, not me."

Calladine couldn't help but wonder why Madison's family hadn't asked about her. She was young, alone in a strange country — surely someone must be curious about what had become of her?

"Is there anyone else we can speak to — a friend perhaps? We don't mind waiting."

"Yes, there is actually. You could talk to Alice Bolshaw. She was Madison's closest friend and she's still here — doing a degree in criminology as it happens."

An amateur sleuth — just what they needed.

"Where do we find her?"

"If you follow the corridor as far as the stairs, you'll find the refectory on your right. Go and have some coffee. I'll find Alice and send her to you."

That wasn't a bad idea. Calladine checked his watch — it had gone lunchtime, but a place like this always had food on the go. As it turned out the refectory was newly refurbished, warm and comfortable. There were a number of students sitting around, chatting and eating, with piped music providing background noise. The food on offer was quite good and relatively cheap. Ruth didn't want anything, but Calladine ordered a bacon sandwich and they both had coffee.

"She must have had somewhere to go, sir — someone to go to. It doesn't make sense to leave here otherwise."

"Nothing about any of this makes much sense yet, Ruth." Calladine squeezed ketchup all over the bacon.

"I don't know how you can. Not after . . . well, after what we've just seen."

"I'm starving, simple as, and this will fill a gap quite nicely."

"Are you the police?" A young woman approached their table.

"Yes. I'm Inspector Calladine and this is Sergeant Bayliss." Calladine smiled.

"Is it true?" Her face was a picture of misery. "Mrs Johnson told me that Maddy is dead."

"I'm afraid Mrs Johnson is right. Are you Alice?" Ruth spoke gently.

The young woman nodded her head, folded her arms and stuck her chin in the air, obviously annoyed about something.

"This is exactly what I warned Maddy about. I knew it, you know. I knew something awful would happen to her. I had a bad feeling when she left. I came to see your lot about her a good few weeks back, but you took no notice. If you had, Madison might still be alive." She stood over them, accusingly. Then she pulled some papers from her bag. "They had the cheek to treat me like a fool. Well, who's looking foolish now? They said I was over reacting, and that she'd turn up. They didn't even ask me to fill out a form or anything."

"Do you know what happened; where Madison went?"

The girl nodded. "Well not exactly, but I know she went off with him — the man she met online. I did try to warn her. I told her she was stupid to get involved with him so soon. I mean he could have been anybody. In a way she only has herself to blame."

"That's a little harsh, Alice." Alice Bolshaw was something of an oddity, Calladine decided. She didn't look much like the other students, who were mostly dressed in jeans, clutching cans of soft drink and generally having a good time hanging out. Alice's clothing was slightly old-fashioned, as well as being immaculate. She was dressed in a pleated skirt and buttoned-up cardigan. She wore no make-up, and her long hair was scraped back, tied in a single thick plait at the back. She looked as if she was something of a cold fish. She obviously didn't suffer fools, and was probably far too serious to relax and enjoy herself. "Involved with whom, Alice? Do you know his name?"

"I just told you. The bloke she met online. Jack, she said his name was. I told your people all this ages ago, but no one listened."

"We're not local police. We're from Leesworth — so we wouldn't necessarily have known about your friend being missing. Do you remember when you went to the police?"

"Yes, I do. It was a few weeks ago; the tenth of October to be precise — before the half-term break. But she wasn't missing then, not in the real sense. I was trying to prevent that. I knew she'd gone, but I still believed she was okay. It was only when she suddenly stopped texting me that I got really worried. Then I knew something was definitely wrong. All along I thought this man she'd taken up with was a bad lot. He was a fast worker — too fast for comfort if you ask me. Goodness knows what he promised Maddy, but it did the trick. I could see the whole thing for what it was, but Maddy couldn't — she just thought I was jealous."

"So where did you think she was?"

"With him: Jack. The precious Jack who was going to solve all her problems and provide her with a life of luxury. Well that's how he must have sold it to her. The silly girl was completely taken in. I tried to talk some sense into her, but in the end she got all shirty and left. Here's her last number." She handed Ruth the papers she'd taken from her bag. Those are the last text messages we exchanged. I printed them out with the dates."

Calladine was impressed. It would have been so easy to delete the texts and forget all about it. "Do you know where this Jack lives, or what he looks like?"

"No. I never actually met him, and Maddy would never answer my questions. She just said he lived somewhere posh and wonderful and had a lot of money. One day she got dressed up and went to meet him for lunch — and I never saw her again. I got the texts telling me what a great time she was having — then nothing."

"This is good work." Ruth scanned through the papers. "Well done."

The young woman sat down beside them. "There is more. Since Maddy's disappearance I've been digging around. I don't want you to think I'm obsessed or anything, but I don't think what happened to Maddy was an isolated case. I suspect that there have been others. I've made a list."

"A list?"

"Yes, Inspector. A list of female students who've simply disappeared for no good reason during the last twelve months." Her tone suggested she wasn't impressed by the amused look on his face. "And don't think I've not asked about them, because I have, and got nowhere. I just don't have the resources or access to them. But I don't harbour these suspicions lightly, and nor should you."

"You're doing a criminology degree. Do you want to be a detective?"

"No, I want to be a profiler. And before you ask, this is not down to my imagination. Just because I spend my time studying criminals doesn't mean I see evil all around me. This is real, Inspector, take my word for it."

"So there have been a few disappearances? But isn't that the way with students at university? They start a course and soon realise it's too much like hard work, not to mention the cost."

"Not these students. Most of them were from the USA, and being sponsored. Maddy had a scholarship from a large corporation in New York. Not a fortune, but enough to get by on. Once she'd qualified they would have employed her, and it was the same with the others. I compiled the list because no one would listen to me. And now Maddy's dead, and I don't think she was the first." She bit her lip thoughtfully.

"What do you think is wrong, Alice? You've obviously put work into this and developed a theory."

"I know what you're thinking; you've hinted as much. You think I'm a criminology student with an overactive imagination. But you're wrong." She spoke with passion. "I think Maddy was taken by a killer — a serial killer." This was said with more than a pinch of bravado. "I think female students here — particularly the ones from the USA — are being targeted. Look. I've highlighted the American students. All were female, and all left without going through any of the formalities or saying goodbye to their friends. Now why would they do that?"

Could she be right? Calladine hoped not. His eyes moved down the list. He was half hoping the name Vida might be there — but it wasn't.

"All these highlighted are American, and no longer here?"

"That's right."

"Thank you, Alice. You can rest assured we will follow this up. I'm not saying you're right — not yet." Calladine reached into his pocket for one of his cards. "Ring me with anything else you discover — anything, even if you think it isn't relevant."

Alice nodded. She was pleased with herself for speaking out like this. "I still have some of Maddy's stuff — most importantly, her laptop. You should take it with you. I can't get into it — it's password protected."

"We have someone back at the station who'll deal with that. It could prove very useful — thanks again."

The 'someone' he had in mind was Imogen. Listening to Alice, and becoming aware of the extent of the research she'd done — he could see that these two young women had a lot in common.

"I've got a lecture very soon, so I'll have to go. If one of you comes with me, I'll give you Maddy's things."

"You go, Ruth. I want to have another word with Joanna Johnson before we leave."

Calladine already suspected their man had murdered more than one woman, so why not look at Alice's list a little closer? Their man had a particular method — the thing with the teeth, the mouth and the tag in the ear. It was possible that he had a favourite hunting ground too, so Alice Bolshaw just might be right. Manchester's colleges were the perfect place to find young women who were alone for the first time in a strange city — impressionable young women, with no family close by.

Calladine went back to Mrs Johnson's office and found her deep in conversation with a young man. He tapped on the half-open door.

"Inspector!" she exclaimed. "Come in — we're finished here."

"Can I use your photocopier?" As he made a copy of Alice's list, he said, "I want to know the addresses and next of kin of all these students. Please. Once you've compiled it, email it to me here. Time is of the essence, so I'd appreciate it if you made this a priority. This is a murder enquiry."

Chapter 11

"Imogen, see what you can do with this." Calladine handed her the laptop. "It belonged to the first dead girl — Vida 5, or to give her her proper name, Madison Benneti. Her friend tells me it's password protected so she can't get into it. I'm particularly interested in the social networking sites she used — emails, any photos you find — that sort of thing."

"Piece of cake."

If anyone could get anything from the laptop, then it was Imogen. It was a skill she excelled at, and it had made her invaluable to the team. Calladine disappeared into his office and sat down at his desk. He needed to think. He needed to sift the information they had so far. But he particularly needed to know the meaning behind that name — Vida.

He logged onto the system and did an internet search. Apparently Vida was a female name and more common in the USA. Now why didn't that surprise him? And where did it lead him? A nutter so obsessed with a woman called Vida that he'd taken to murdering other women and tagging them with her name. But why? Why call them all by her name, and what had happened to the original Vida?

He sifted through the file and took out a photograph of Madison Benneti. She'd been young, slim, with long fair hair and, of course, American. Was he seeking out women who looked like Vida?

"Sir! I've just had a call from Julian. He's got a name for the second one — Vida 3."

"How come?"

"Her DNA was on record," Ruth told him. "She was arrested in a drugs bust two years ago at a student house in Manchester."

"Who is she?"

"Serena Hall — and guess what?"

Calladine's mouth pulled into a grim smile. "Don't tell me — she was a student in Manchester, and American."

"Got it in one. From New York actually — somewhere called Queens."

"So now we've got a little more than just Alice's theories to work with." He picked up the phone. "I want to speak to Joanna Johnson. This is Inspector Calladine from Leesworth Police."

He gestured for Ruth to sit while he waited to be put through. "You're still looking peaky. Not coming down with something, are you?"

"No, just tired."

"Mrs Johnson, It's looking highly likely that someone is targeting students from the USA. I could do with you going through that list and letting me have the information today. I'd also like you to check if you had a student called Serena Hall, and if so, would you email me a photo of her as soon as you can? You might want to have a few words with the other American students and warn them to be careful. Particularly about social networking sites, and taking up with men they don't know."

"So this is real — something more than just Alice Bolshaw's ramblings?"

"It is. If anything, we should all be grateful to that young woman. She's done us a great favour by noticing what was going on."

"I'll get onto it straight away. I'll commandeer some more staff to help." She paused. "This is awful. Alice has been badgering me for weeks, and I've taken no notice. I'll get back to you quickly. Don't worry, Inspector."

"Seems to have shaken her up a bit. So what have we got, Ruth?"

"A serial murderer — and on our patch too by the look of things. The body in the pile-up was one thing, but leaving the second one at the Leesworth undertakers was too much of a coincidence."

"I think you're right. He's local but he's hunting in student land."

"I think that's because he's after a particular type. He wants young women from the USA who look a certain way — young women he calls Vida. And we know, because of the numbers, that there are bound to be more. But what's he done with the rest of them, sir? Where are they being kept? Serena Hall's been dead a while, so where's she been? And we have to ask ourselves what's prompted him to get rid of her now?'

"It has to be something major — something that's forced him to change his usual method of operation."

He rubbed his eyes. He was tired; too much to think about. His mind wouldn't let go, so he could get no rest. It'd been a pig of a week, starting with his mother's funeral. And now this little lot.

"You look as bad as I feel, Tom. You need a break."

"I've got a lot of things rumbling around in my head. Sometimes I think I'm my own worst enemy. I really could do with being able to relax more, but the questions and theories are relentless."

"Perhaps you need a night out — a few beers. Why don't you ask the lads or even better, speak to Monika?"

"I'm a bloody fool, Ruth. I should never have messed things up with her. Do you think it's too late?"

"Well, I don't think the little fling you had with the blonde has helped. But if you're feeling brave then why not try? Swallow your pride; mend a few fences."

"But I was such an ass. What was I doing? That woman wasn't much older than Zoe. What do you think — honestly?"

"I think you should try. Give it your best shot. She can only tell you to piss off. Why not do it now?"

"Do I have to?"

"Yes, I really think you do. It might make you feel better to know you've tried, if nothing else."

"I'll ring her tonight."

"I don't think this is something you should do over the phone either, and what's wrong with now?"

"Too much to do, that's what." An email appeared in his inbox. "This is from Mrs Johnson."

He sent the attached photo straight to the printer. "Get the team together next door, Ruth. Let's look at what we've got." He pushed the printout over to Ruth. "Remind you of anyone?"

"Is that Serena? Because if it is, then she's scarily like Madison." Ruth shuddered and took the photo from him. "I'll pin it on the board and tell the guys."

"Julian says he'll have something on the latest body within twenty-four hours, sir," Rocco told Calladine as he walked into the main office. "He says she was in soil for a while, so he's doing an analysis. He'll try to pinpoint where she was buried if he can."

Good idea — if the science could be that precise.

"Right, folks." The inspector took up his position in front of the incident board. "It looks highly likely that we're dealing with a serial killer. The victims so far are young women who bear a striking resemblance to each other, and are from the USA. We have two victims: Madison Benneti and Serena Hall. Madison Benneti's friend, Alice Bolshaw, drew up a list of other American students who have disappeared from the university leaving no forwarding address and giving no explanations. Serena Hall is on that list. So I'm having their addresses and phone numbers dug out as we speak, and once I get them they'll all need checking out. I want to know the whereabouts of every person on that list. Is that clear?"

"Do we know if there have been any enquiries from the police in the States?" Imogen asked.

"No. The university isn't aware of any."

"Why do you reckon that is, sir? Surely if a youngster goes missing in a foreign country, there's all sorts of investigations."

"I think it's down to how he chooses them. With any luck, Madison's laptop will prove helpful. Alice told Ruth that our man found Madison on a social networking site and then started a relationship with her. I think he goes not only for a physical type, but also for women who are alone — with no nosey family in the background."

"I've cracked the login password already, sir." Imogen spoke up. "So with a bit of luck I'll get into her inbox quite soon."

"Then with a little more luck we'll have something." Calladine paused and shook his head. "The bastard doesn't make it clean. He keeps the girls somewhere and tortures them over time. He removes some of their teeth and stitches the mouth shut, and with Madison there was evidence of persistent rape. In fact the girl was in the early stages of pregnancy and someone had attempted an abortion."

"Looks like he blamed someone else for her condition, then," Rocco suggested. "Perhaps he did those things and killed her because he believed she'd been unfaithful."

"Nice theory, Rocco, but the dates don't match. Given the length of time she'd been missing from college, the pregnancy must have been down to our man. We've got DNA, so when we get him we'll know for sure."

"In that case he's got a real screw loose."

"I think we'd all agree with that, Rocco. A gold-plated screw loose, in fact."

DCI George Jones came into the office and stood in the doorway while Calladine spoke.

"We need to know how many more we could be looking at. We think at least another three, but we can't be sure. I'm going to divvy up a list of phone numbers — they're all in the States but I'm afraid they will need checking — every last one. Me and Ruth will visit the college again and get a formal statement from Alice Bolshaw. Ask her if she recalls anything else — particularly if she knew Serena Hall. Imogen — the minute you get anything from that laptop get it up on the board — photos, copies of emails — anything and everything that might help us find our man."

He paused. They were scribbling away in their notebooks. They all realised the urgency of this. This bastard needed catching before more bodies turned up.

"Tom, a word if you've finished." Jones barked the order, without so much as a glance at the others.

"Definite charisma bypass if you ask me," Rocco whispered to Imogen. "I don't know how the guv stands it. It should be him in that job, not DCI Charming over there."

"Central haven't received your statement yet, Tom. You should really get that one wrapped up quickly."

Tom Calladine shot the DCI a disapproving look. The fact that he was Ray Fallon's cousin was not common knowledge in the nick. Only the DCI and Ruth knew. So he didn't want the DCI shouting his mouth off. The others on his team would ask those awkward questions he didn't want to answer.

"Yes, sir, I'll get onto it. We do have a lot on. In fact I could do with a minute or two to fill you in."

He followed Jones back to his office.

* * *

"Why does the boss have to give a statement to Central?" Rocco asked Ruth. "Has he been up to something we should know about?"

"Nothing that concerns you, Rocco, so just get on with what you're supposed to be doing." She passed him a card with Alice Bolshaw's number on it. "Give her a ring and tell her we'll be in to see her later today."

"Not sure what's going on, or what it has to do with the boss. But what I do know is that Central has its hands full at the moment. There was a gangland shooting earlier in the week. The only witness in a major case was shot and killed. Nasty business and it's got them all edgy and looking for someone to blame. But someone tipped the bad guys off, so the push is on to find out who that was. The whisper has it that it might even have been a cop. So why they'd want to see the boss is lost on me. Surely they can't think that he's involved somehow — do you?"

"Don't be daft, Rocco. What would Calladine know about the likes of Ray Fallon and his crew?" Ruth tried to close the discussion down.

Chapter 12

She was such an innocent. An innocent unsuspecting fool. Just what he needed. He'd told her to take the train from Victoria to a quiet little station two stops from Huddersfield. He'd arranged to meet her at the bus stop outside. She hadn't even questioned the plans when he'd phoned her. She'd simply laughed that light tinkle of a laugh she had, and enthused about their weekend together.

He was beginning to wonder whether she was such a good idea after all. Vida was never that gullible. She was mature, sensible, and would've seen through his subterfuge in a second. So if Patsy Lumis wasn't right for him, then how to deal with her? Not nicely — that was for sure. He'd take what he wanted and have some fun. His kind of fun — and she wouldn't enjoy it, not one little bit. But what did he care?

He'd checked out the bus stop and the road for a hundred yards either way. There were no cameras. He'd park up, get her in and bring her back to his place as quickly as possible.

It was a good plan. He couldn't see any problems. In the night, the street was particularly dark because the nearby street light was blinking off and on — even better. He sat in his van and waited anxiously for the train. He hadn't bothered to change, and was still wearing his work clothes. She'd turn her cute little nose up, but that didn't matter now. He could sweet-talk her round.

Once he got her back he'd treat her like a proper lady — for a short while. He'd prepared food — of sorts. Some small savoury pastries from the bakers in Leesdon, and a bottle of wine. They'd eat and she'd drink — then he'd have her. He'd laced the wine with GHB. It was his favourite because of the effect it had. He'd also added some diazepam for good measure — he wanted it to work quickly. He wanted her sleepy and sexually uninhibited. He could feel his loins stirring already at the thought of what he'd do to her. He'd have her straight away — rough and hard, in the isolation of his special place. She could scream all she liked and no one would hear. Serve her right — stupid cow!

He heard the train pull in and a couple of people ran up the steps and into the station. He waited, clicking his fingers with impatience. Where was she? Then he saw her. The bitch was talking to someone — an older woman. What was she doing? He didn't want anyone to remember seeing her — so what now? He thumped his fist on the steering wheel, making the horn blast, and her head shot round. She'd seen him.

He watched her smile at the woman and wave goodbye, and then teeter towards him in those stupid heels she wore, dragging her suitcase behind her.

"Friend of yours?"

Patsy Lumis shook her head and attempted to lift her case into the van.

"Aren't you going to help me, Jack? Do you want me to put it in the back?"

He nodded, jumped out, hastily opened the back doors and threw it in. She wasn't playing the game — but she would, very soon, he tried to reassure himself.

"Do you know that woman?"

"No, we just started talking. She was in America last year and we were swapping sightseeing stories, that's all. It's no biggie, Jack. She was just, like, some random woman."

He shot her an angry look and pulled away. He had to calm down or this wouldn't work. Even she might twig what he was really up to, and he couldn't have that.

"Sorry, babe. For one awful moment back there, I thought you might have brought someone with you."

"Silly Jack." She rubbed his arm. "That would spoil our fun, and I wouldn't want to do that. I want to spend this whole weekend getting to know you — just us two together. We don't need anyone else."

How true that was. He smiled at her and turned the radio on low. The music was relaxing and he needed to be calm for the next bit.

They drove for a few miles, leaving the town and train station behind them. They wound their way through the pitch dark, along the narrow roads that led through the Pennines and down into Leesworth. Jack knew these roads well, every last inch of them, and he knew exactly which route to take so he wouldn't be seen.

"Thought we could do something romantic. I've got some food and wine for us back at mine. We can relax and celebrate our first night together."

Patsy Lumis was delighted. "I can't wait to be with you, Jack. You know what I mean. You're such a hot guy."

"Here, help yourself." He handed her a wine bottle and a glass. "Fill your boots. Get yourself in the mood."

Patsy giggled and poured a large helping of wine, filling the beaker nearly to the top.

"Good stuff that." He smiled. "It's not your bog-standard supermarket plonk."

She sipped delicately, her eyes sparkling in the half-light of the van.

"You're spoiling me," she trilled. "I love things like this, so spontaneous and romantic." She leaned over and kissed his cheek.

"Don't be shy. Drink up, there's plenty more."

He saw her reach for the bottle again, out of the corner of his eye. It wouldn't be long; he'd planned it well. She wouldn't be able to finish this one — she'd be out cold.

"You're not having any wine?"

"Better not — I'm driving. But you have what you want."

"When we get to yours I can cook, if you like. I'm quite good, I really am. I'll make you one of my signature dishes. You'll love it."

"We'll see." He stroked her hair as she began to yawn. The cocktail of drugs was working — so they should, he'd used enough of them.

"Whoa . . . I feel kind of weird, sort of sleepy and numb."

"You're probably tired. Look, it's a good few miles yet. Just lean back in the seat and snooze for a while."

She nodded, her eyes closed and her head sagged forward.

This was far too easy. He picked up her arm and watched it flop back as he released it. She didn't even groan — she was completely out of it.

Half an hour or so later he pulled up outside his special place. It was dark and secluded and there was no chance of being seen. He hauled her out and laid her on the ground while he unlocked the door. Then he hauled her from the car and dragged her in. She was inert and heavy, and he was hot and panting by the time he got her to his room. But she was worth it. He was excited beyond measure. He tore wildly at the clothing on her lower body. Her skirt, tights and finally her knickers were all thrown aside and he bent her legs, spreading them wide. She was slim with shapely thighs and smooth creamy skin. A tidy mound of dark fluff between her legs — perfect. She didn't stir.

He was frantic. His fingers flew to his jeans and he fumbled for a moment with the belt and then pulled them off. Kneeling down, he growled like a beast and grasped his penis, thrusting it deep into her. No foreplay, no gentleness. He pounded into her relentlessly, again and again, filled with pure hate.

* * *

Calladine had fallen asleep on his sofa again and woke with a start when he heard the front door open.

"Zoe?" Is that you?"

"Yep, Tom. Sorry I'm late. I know I said I'd be home to eat, but something came up."

He looked at the clock on the mantle — nearly ten. He'd had no tea. He'd got back from the nick, sat down with a drop of scotch, and that was that.

"Working late?"

"No. I've been eating out with Jo. We went to that Italian place in Hopecross. The food's great and reasonable too. You should try it sometime."

"You and Jo are spending a lot of time together — you practically work with each other, too."

"Not a problem. I like Jo."

Calladine saw that look on her face, the one she had when there was something on her mind. "Want to say something?" he asked.

She paused and looked at her father. "I suppose I should say something. You'll have to know sooner or later."

"Know what?

"About Jo — well, about me and Jo."

"Why, what have you two been up to?" There was something about the way she'd said that, something about the look on her face.

"Jo and I are fond of each other. Tom — we sort of clicked right away. You know how it is."

Did he? He wasn't sure what she was getting at. Did she mean 'click' in the sort of way he was familiar with — the 'fancying someone' sort of way?

"You're struggling, aren't you?" She shook her head. "Jo and I are happy to be together. You know . . . together?" She stood watching him, her hands on her hips. "I was hoping you'd guess, Tom. I've tried to give you enough clues. And you call yourself a detective!"

Was she saying what he thought she was saying?

"'You and your estate agent friend, you're . . . ?"

"Yes, Tom — gay. I'm gay, we're gay — a gay couple in fact. And I'm not going to apologise or explain myself, so don't make an issue of it. But it doesn't bother you, does it?"

Did it? Truthfully, Tom Calladine wasn't sure. He'd have to give it some thought, mull it over for a while. In the meantime he shrugged as casually as he could, rose up off the sofa and kissed her cheek.

"Be happy, love, that's all I want for you. I'm envious in a way. Your love life seems pretty simple in comparison to mine. I'm still debating what to do about Monika. Ruth says I should go and see her, apologise for being such an ass, but I don't think she'll go for it. Too much water under the bridge." He sighed.

"Is that what's been bothering you?" Zoe seemed relieved that he hadn't reacted negatively to finding out she was gay.

"Not only that. There's work as well. We've got a particularly nasty case on our hands at present, and I suspect it's only going to get worse."

"You have to let go sometimes, Tom. Taking up with Monika again sounds like a good idea. It'd get you out and take your mind off things. Is anything else bothering you?"

"My bloody cousin's giving me grief at work. He's responsible for killing a witness who was due to testify against him, and he's had the damn nerve to use me as his alibi."

"Is he telling the truth? Was he where he says he was? Can you vouch for him?"

"Yes, I can, and that's the bloody problem."

"Then he can't have done it. Or can he?"

"Oh, yes he can; he's a sneaky bastard. I just have to work out how, that's all."

"Perhaps I can help."

"Are you sure you want to? I thought you liked him. You gave me the impression that you couldn't wait to get to know him better."

"I'm not that stupid. I'm a solicitor, Tom. Okay, so I might deal with house conveyancing, but I do know one or two criminal lawyers. After what you said I asked around, and you're right: he's a complete and utter bastard, and not someone to meddle with."

Calladine laughed and handed her a glass. "I'll drink to that." He reached for the scotch. "But how could he be at the church and shooting a man at the same time?" He poured her a measure of whiskey.

"Well he couldn't, could he? He must have done the deed either before the funeral or after," she replied.

"But he didn't. A fairly accurate time of death has been established, and that puts him in church — along with his goons. Even allowing for a short window either way, I still can't make it work."

"You're not thinking hard enough, Tom."

"I'm thinking so damn hard it put me to sleep."

"They are sure it was Fallon's doing?"

"Yep. He was seen dumping the body from a bridge over the M62. Him, his goons and that posh motor he drives."

"Well isn't that enough?"

"No. He'll wriggle out of it. What with my alibi, and somehow managing to prove that whoever saw them on the bridge was short-sighted or something, he'll walk. He's recently walked away from one sure bet — the drugs bust central thought they'd got him on. Not even worth the effort."

"So we're back to the original question; how did he do it?"

Zoe disappeared into the kitchen and Calladine heard her putting the kettle on. "Scotch isn't for me. Do you fancy a cup of tea?"

He shook his head. He'd stick with the scotch.

Zoe put her head around the kitchen door. "Of course there is a way he could have done it. He could have shot the guy and shoved him in the boot of that huge car he drives. The body could have been there all through the service. Have you thought of that?"

No, he hadn't — and it wasn't a bad idea. But how to prove it?

Chapter 13

Day Five

"Tom! Can I have a word please?" DCI Jones strode into the incident room.

"What can I do for you, sir?" Calladine looked round from the board, which he had been studying intently.

"The States, Tom — this list. I'm thinking of the cost of all those phone calls. Are they really necessary?"

He was at it again, the penny-pinching fool!

"I'm afraid they are, sir. That list is students from the university who may be missing. At least two students from the States have ended up dead on our patch, so we need to know how many more we could be looking at."

"I appreciate that, but couldn't we leave the spadework to the university? They were their students after all."

"Yes but the bodies are ours, sir. And when others turn up they will be ours too." He spoke as calmly as he could, trying hard not to lose it. Tom Calladine was ready to blow, and if the DCI didn't get out of his face soon . . .

Jones sighed. "Budgets, Tom. We only have so much money to play with. This could blow our phone bill sky high."

"Can't be helped I'm afraid. At the very least, the families of the dead girls need to know."

"Okay, contact them, but leave the others for the time being. I'll sort something out. Something cheaper."

And exactly how was he going to do that? Calladine inhaled deeply in an attempt to calm his anger. What did Jones imagine they were all doing here? That man had spent so long tucked in that little office of his that he'd lost all comprehension of what really went on.

Ruth was sat at her desk, shaking her head and swearing under her breath. "Bloody idiot. Does he think we do this for the fun of it? We have to spend money sometimes. I bet he's not seen the overtime bill yet, has he, sir?"

"Now now, Sergeant Bayliss. Take it easy. Let's not get riled, and less of the cheek . . . We'll give him until lunchtime and then we'll crack on with the calls regardless. What we all really want is an end to this. He's with us on that one, surely?"

"Monika?"

"Not yet, and please don't go on about it. I've enough on right now."

"Coward! What's happened to you?"

"Sleep — or rather the lack of it — that's what happened. I'll sort it, I promise."

"You can tell me about it on the way to the university. And don't go thinking I'll let you wimp out, because I won't. You need that woman, Tom Calladine."

She was probably right, but he didn't feel like dissecting his love life right now.

"Give me a minute. I want to check if Julian got anywhere with the CCTV from the undertakers." He picked up the phone and tapped in the forensic scientist's number. All he got was his answer service.

"He must be out, or busy."

"Or even both."

"Okay. We'll get off to Manchester and check with him on our way back."

He went into his office and grabbed his coat.

"I'm in, sir!" Imogen announced as he and Ruth made to leave. "I've got access to the social media site Madison used, so now I can look at her posts. I'll have a look around, see what I can find and fill you in later. One thing though — and this could be vital. He was pushing Madison. He said he had someone else and he'd dump her if she didn't make her mind up about him. He said the new girl was already lined up and keen — someone she knew. He was getting at her — taunting her for her indecision. It seems Madison got very jealous and threatened to sort the girl out. It might be important to find out who this other girl is, sir."

One after the other, then. One on the go and one in the wings. He had to put an end to this.

"Try and find out her name — anything to help us identify her before it's too late. If you get anywhere, then ring me."

"Alice might know, sir," Ruth suggested.

Ah, the all-knowing Alice. He didn't want to rely on her too much. She was far too intense for him. A young girl like her should be out enjoying herself not poking around compiling lists — even if it was an enormous help.

"This new girl should take precedence, don't you think? We should speak to her friends and make sure she's okay before we chase after folk who knew Serena."

She was right. This other girl could be in danger.

* * *

"You might be feeling rough but you don't look so ragged around the edges today."

"I don't know. All the abuse I have to put up with, not only from Jones but now from you as well . . . But I suppose I did sleep a little better last night. I had an interesting conversation with Zoe, and she helped me to figure something out. She thinks Fallon might have brought the body to the funeral in the boot of his car. I just have to work out how to prove it. Oh — and did you know that she's a lesbian?" He still hadn't made his mind up about that one.

"Yes, I guessed actually."

"She told you?"

"No — I said I guessed. Come on, sir, I really expected you to twig. She's made no secret of it."

Calladine was mystified. He'd had no idea until his daughter had told him. "How does that work then? How did you know?"

"I guess my *gaydar* is a little sharper than yours, that's all. You don't have a problem with it, do you? I didn't have you down as homophobic."

"That's because I'm not, and it isn't a problem, not really. It's just that when Zoe turned up like she did, and I'd got used to the idea of having a daughter, I allowed myself to indulge a little. For the first time ever I started to think about an extended family — grandkids even."

"Tom Calladine! You old softie. Have you told Zoe how you feel?"

"God no, I wouldn't know where to start."

"She might not even want kids; but you should ask her. It is the twenty-first century, you know. Gay couples get married, and they also have kids. There are ways and means."

* * *

When they reached the university they made their way to Joanna Johnson's office. They now needed to know who Madison Benneti's friends were, apart from Alice — particularly the Americans.

"I'm not sure. They do meet up, our overseas students. There are a number of groups and social events they go to," the tutor said.

"Who would know, then?" Ruth asked.

"Well, I suppose you need to speak to Alice again." Joanna Johnson sighed. "Believe me, she'll be only too pleased to help. She came and had a word with me after you spoke to her. She wants to do a period of work experience with your team."

Work experience — that was a new one. As far back as Calladine could remember, no one had ever put themselves up for that little treat.

"I'll get her to meet you. Refectory again?"

"Late breakfast? Or have you eaten?"

"Not that organised I'm afraid. I left early and Zoe had already gone."

"Surely you don't expect her to run after you, sir? Make breakfast . . . Her job is every bit as demanding as yours, you know."

"She does conveyancing. How demanding can that be?"

"Very tricky job. All those impatient house-buyers wanting things to move faster, irate phone calls and having to get all those searches right. Give me police work any day."

"Don't be so sarcastic. I could go off you, Ruth Bayliss. You've become far too smart-arsed for your own good, if you ask me."

They queued at the counter along with the students and helped themselves to a selection of what was on offer. Well Calladine did, but when it came to it, all Ruth could stomach was tea and toast.

"More bacon, more sauce — don't know how you can."

"You could once. What's happened to you?"

"A girl has to watch her figure. I only have to look at food these days and I pile it on."

Calladine looked her up and down. That couldn't be right. In fact, to him she looked as if she'd lost a little weight. It showed mostly in her face. She was looking prettier somehow. Was that the Jake effect? Or the fact that she'd grown her hair longer? What was it about women? Give them a few weeks and they could completely change their appearance. Whereas men — well, they remained stubbornly the same. He certainly did. A short, no-nonsense haircut and the colour left to do its own thing — which these days, was defaulting to grey. As for his weight, it hadn't changed in years, regardless of what he insulted his stomach with.

"You're back." Alice hurried over to their table and sat down, looking uncharacteristically animated. "I was hoping I'd see you again. I want to ask you something."

"Yes, Mrs Johnson told us," Calladine replied between mouthfuls of bacon butty. "But working with us might not be such a good idea — not yet anyway. Not with your personal involvement in the current case."

"But that's why I want to. I can help; I know I can, Inspector."

"It's not pleasant, Alice," Ruth warned. "You'd see things; have access to things that you'll find painful. You and Madison were friends, remember? So it would be bound to upset you."

"I could turn all that off — I really could."

There was something about this young woman that made that believable. Calladine couldn't put his finger on it but she had a distinctly cold, clinical side — a bit like Julian.

"I want this — I want to help. I want to get stuck into something real, not some textbook mock-up. It would help me on my course, and possibly form the basis of my dissertation. If I took a look at what you've got so far I could have a go at profiling — I'd love that."

"I'll think about it." Calladine had never been too keen on the idea of profiling — too many generalities. "There are formalities, but I'll see what I can organise."

Alice gave them both a rare smile. "What can I do for you today?"

"We know that Madison was afraid her murderer might turn his attention to someone else. He threatened to do this in their online chats. Can you recall if she was angry with anyone, or jealous? It would probably be someone her age, with her physical build and from the States."

"Madison was a very jealous person — it was a weakness. I kept telling her about it. It didn't have to be about much either. She wasn't really a friendly girl. She was friendly with me, but then she didn't see me as any kind of threat — too geeky. She would have been better off paying more attention to her studies. She could be very nasty to the other girls. She saw all females as rivals — stupid, if you ask me."

"Was there anyone in particular that she talked about before she disappeared — anyone she criticised?"

"I suppose she wasn't happy about Patsy — Patsy Lumis. And, yes, they were quite similar really, not just in age and interests, but in the way they looked too. They had a bit of a set-to in the refectory. I remember Madison called Patsy all sorts of names. She never said what it was about though — well not to me anyway."

Calladine gave Ruth a nod. "Where can we find Patsy?"

"At this time of day she'll be in the library. I'll take you."

The two detectives followed Alice out across the main reception area and into the newly-equipped modern library. It occupied a large area, and had an IT suite off to one side. Alice looked around for a moment, and then gestured towards a girl seated in front of a monitor.

"'She's not here but that's Anna Morris, Patsy's friend. She'll know where she is."

"Thanks, Alice. Look — leave the work thing with me and I'll be in touch soon, okay?"

Alice nodded and left them to it.

* * *

"Anna Morris?" Ruth flashed her warrant card. "I'm DS Bayliss and this is DI Calladine. We're from Leesworth CID, and we wonder if you'd mind answering a few questions?"

Anna's eyes darted from one detective to the other.

"What's this about? I haven't done anything wrong — well not that I know of."

"We just want to ask you about your friend Patsy. Is she around?"

"Well, no. She's gone off somewhere for a day or two. Is she in trouble?"

Calladine sat down on the empty seat beside the girl. He had a bad feeling. This was how it started. "When did she go, Anna?"

"Last night. She has a new boyfriend and she's gone to stay with him. He's a little odd if you ask me. He gave her a load of funny instructions to get to his place, down to what train to get and what station to get off at. So she went — packed her stuff and left. I wasn't happy — I mean she hardly knows him. She can't have seen him above twice, and now she's off spending time at his."

"Have you met him?"

"Yes, once — in the pub the other night. That was the first time Patsy'd met him too. They'd been chatting online for ages before he asked to see her. She fell for his chat-up lines big time. She's such a fool when it comes to men. He turned up dressed to the nines. He bought us some drinks and we swapped a few words, then I left them to it."

"What pub was that?" Ruth asked.

"The one under the railway arch a few yards up the road from here. We always go in there. It's not much but it's popular with the students."

"Could you describe him, Anna? It's important. It's possible that Patsy could be in trouble."

"What's she done?"

"Nothing. But the man she's with could be dangerous."

"I thought he was creepy that night. It wasn't anything he said — it's hard to explain really, it was just a feeling. I told Patsy but she wouldn't listen. I mean, who goes off with some random man after knowing him less than a week?" Her voice rose to a wail.

"Can you come back to the station with us? We'll get our e-fit people to sit with you and see if we can get a reasonable likeness. You can give us all the details you recall about that night too."

"Did she have her own laptop?" Calladine chipped in.

Anna nodded. "It's in her room. I have a key; I can get it if you want."

"Ruth, you go with Anna and I'll go tell Joanna Johnson what we're doing. If you come with us now, we'll have you back by the afternoon."

Calladine took his mobile from his coat pocket and rang Imogen. "Have you got a name for the other girl yet?"

"I can only get a first name, sir. From what he wrote it looks like she was called Patsy. He goes on about how lovely she is, and how easy it would be to go for her instead of Madison."

"It looks very likely he's done just that — not instead of, but as well as. Look, Imogen, can you have one of the e-fit boys standing by? I'm bringing someone in who can give us a description. We've found a young woman who's actually met this creep."

113

"You think he's taken another one then? Another one of ours?" Joanna Johnson's eyes became wide with horror when Calladine told her what had happened.

"Possibly, but we need to investigate further. In the meantime, if Patsy Lumis turns up, let me know straight away. I'll send another of my team down to speak to Serena Hall's friends. I don't have time to see them today because it's more important that I get back to the station and speak to Anna. Don't forget what I advised about speaking to your students. By tomorrow it'll hit the press, so I suggest you get in there first."

Chapter 14

They had an image. Anna Morris had been able to give a reasonable description of the young man she'd met in the pub two nights ago. But they still had no proper name — just 'Jack.'

"It's time to call in the press. We no longer have a choice. You know how I feel about those harpies, but they could help — and right now we need all the help we can get. If we get this image circulated, particularly around Leesworth, it could pay dividends."

"You'd better clear it with Jones first."

"As long as it doesn't cost it'll be fine."

"The travel instructions he gave Patsy are weird," she said, reading through the statement. "Why send her to the other side of the Pennines? Why not just get off the train in Leesdon?"

"He didn't want to be seen. There are cameras at Leesdon Station and all down the High Street. He's clever. He studied his route, so I doubt we'll get anything, but we'll go take a look anyway."

"It takes about forty-five minutes from Manchester Victoria. I wonder if she spoke to anyone? We could ask — include it in the press briefing; ask for anyone to come forward who might have seen her, or struck up a conversation."

Ruth's idea wasn't bad. Calladine left the incident room and went to find DCI Jones. He should tell him how things were progressing, and what he intended to do. Calladine also needed to know what Jones had decided about the phone calls to the States.

"Frankly it's not on, Tom. Can't allow them all I'm afraid. Far too costly."

"That's stupid, sir. We know there are others, and we could do with knowing which of those young women are safe at home and which aren't."

"Not our problem. Try going through the embassy — they can do the work. Then if the authorities in the States ask, we'll give them what we know — that's all I can do."

The man was a first-class fool. Going through the American embassy would take ages. One way or another, Calladine decided he'd get the information he wanted.

"The press briefing's arranged for tomorrow morning, sir. And Alice Bolshaw's been on the phone. She wants to know if you've made a decision yet."

Joyce's head came up from amidst her paperwork. "That the young woman Ruth said was looking for work experience?"

Calladine nodded. "But, given she was Madison Benneti's friend, I'm not keen. Can you imagine what her reaction will be when she sees that?" He nodded at the board, which was now covered in grisly pictures of the two bodies. "No, I don't think so. Not while this case is ongoing."

"Well if you change your mind, sir, I'll take her. I've a pile of simple routine stuff I can give her to do."

He'd think about it, but even working with Joyce, there was no avoiding the hideous photos on that damn board.

"When do you want to go look at the railway station, sir? It's getting late, so do you want to leave it until tomorrow?"

"Might be better to weigh things up in daylight, and the press release will have gone out by lunchtime tomorrow. If it brings anyone in who saw her get off the train, then we can meet them there — get the full picture."

"Rocco has gone to get the CCTV footage from the pub, and ask a few questions. We'll give it to Julian and see what he comes up with. Imogen — would you make sure Julian knows what Patsy Lumis looks like, so that he can log anyone she spoke to?"

* * *

Ruth was pleased to put the drive to Slaithwaite off until the next day. She had one or two bits and pieces to see to, and then she'd be off home. Jake was coming round and they needed to talk. It was make or break time for their relationship.

"I think I'll call it a day. See you all in the morning!" Calladine reached for his coat.

"With any luck you'll get that 'downtime' that's proving so elusive, sir. A bite to eat, a warm fire and a drop of good scotch — the perfect evening," Ruth smiled.

If only her evening could be so enjoyable. She sighed. Was it all worth it? Could she survive without the job if she had to choose between it and Jake? Financially, she could; Ruth was not a spender — she saved, and had done since she'd been a child. She'd inherited money when her parents had died. No, it wasn't the money she needed — it was the job itself. She loved it.

Jake didn't understand. He couldn't get his head round how she could be so into chasing lunatics and apprehending killers. Mind you he didn't understand her hobby either. According to him it took her away far too often. She had been planning a trip to the Isle of Lewis in the Hebrides, birdwatching, well raptor watching really, but he wasn't keen. If she wanted time away he'd prefer to go somewhere warm — together.

* * *

Zoe was at home with Jo. Not that Calladine minded — not really. But it meant that the downtime would have to wait a while. They had music playing — alien noises filled his sitting room, and Jo was singing at the top of her voice. Both girls looked at each other and laughed as he appeared in the doorway.

"Oops — thought you'd be late." Zoe turned the volume down. "Hope you don't mind, but we thought we'd eat here for change — spend some time with you." His daughter smiled.

Did that smack of wanting something? News to reveal that he might not like? Calladine didn't have much experience of fatherhood, but he was a fast learner.

"I've cooked," she announced. "Well — Jo has, and it's one of her specialities — spaghetti bolognaise."

"Made the way my granny used to make it. She was half Italian and practically brought me up."

There was an appetising smell coming from his kitchen. She was telling the truth then. The log burner had been stoked up, making the small cottage warm and cosy. This was a much better homecoming than the empty house he was used to.

"You look fed up, Mr Calladine." Jo gave him a sympathetic smile. "Is something bothering you? I hope it's not us being here."

"No — definitely not you. But something's usually bothering me; work mostly — and please, call me Tom. 'Mr Calladine' just doesn't sit right."

"Work?"

"That and my DCI — penny-pinching sod that he is. I need to make some phone calls to the States — to check on the whereabouts of a number of young women, but he won't allow it because of the cost. How in this world he expects us to get the job done — well . . . it beggars belief. Then, of course, there's my murdering rogue of a cousin."

"Perhaps I could help — well not with the cousin thing. I don't do families. But I do come from the States, and I have a friend — a policeman who works for the NYPD. I'm sure if I asked him he'd make the enquiries for you."

"Won't he be too busy? They must have quite a workload in New York."

"You're not wrong! He's based in Queens — a borough of New York — and there's never a dull moment. But he won't mind, Devon's one of the good guys."

"Devon? Is that his surname?"

"No. His name is Devon DeAngelo. Devon's his first name."

"Isn't the name a little flamboyant for a detective?"

"Not where I come from." She laughed. "You'd like him, he's a cool guy."

"Serena Hall — one of the girls — came from Queens."

"Then Devon has a vested interest; so much the better. I'll ring him and set up a meeting. Once that's done you can speak to him on Skype."

That wasn't a bad idea at all. They could use Skype at work too. That'd cut out the costs completely, and they'd finally be entering the twenty-first century!

Jo checked her watch. "Just after six here, so it'll be about twelve noon in the US. I'll ring him later. He'll be working now."

She was turning out to be okay. She had contacts — ones he could use. And judging from the smell coming from the kitchen, she could cook too.

"That's very good of you, Jo. I appreciate the help."

"Wait and see what Devon comes up with first. He's okay; he'll do what he can. Here's his email." She scribbled it on a card. "Do you guys want to eat now?"

* * *

She could see lights twinkling in the darkness. Patsy Lumis squinted slightly, trying to make out what they were; candles, she thought. There were dozens of them all around the room and they gave off a sweet aroma — roses. She tried to raise herself up off whatever she was lying on. It wasn't easy. Her head hurt, and every muscle in her body demanded rest. She was lying on an old, lumpy mattress on the floor. Why was that? At the very least she expected to wake up in Jack's bed. Why had he left her here like this?

It took a little effort, but she got groggily to her feet. Most of her clothes had gone — well, from the waist down they had. Patsy looked for something to wrap around herself but couldn't see anything. She hauled at the hem of her blouse, trying to pull it down over her hips. She wasn't cold; there was heating somewhere. She couldn't see a fire, so radiators perhaps. But where was Jack?

He'd rendered her unconscious and taken her clothes. But why? As she took a few tentative steps, she realised that she was terribly sore between her legs — and then she understood. They must have had sex, rough sex, and more than once from the way she felt. Why would he do that? Why would he drug her? Surely he must have realised that she was more than happy to sleep with him. Why else would she have come away with him in the first place? The questions accelerated the panic.

She tried to rationalise her situation, perhaps this was some sort of game. Perhaps he'd appear any second and make everything right. But the sinking feeling in the pit of her stomach was saying something else. This was no game. This was horribly serious, and she needed to get out.

Patsy Lumis felt her way around the room. The candles didn't emit enough light for her to see her surroundings properly. She took hold of one and carefully walked around the perimeter. The room was a narrow oblong and the walls were stone. There was the mattress on the stone flags, but no carpet. The only piece of furniture was what looked like an old dentist's chair in the far corner. There was nothing else. She shuddered; she hated going to the dentist. She opened a wall cupboard above the chair and shuddered again — dental instruments, a whole array of them in gleaming steel. Where the hell was she?

"You really are a nosey girl, aren't you, Vida?"

The voice seemed to come from the far wall. Was there a door there? She hadn't heard anyone come in.

"Jack! Is that you? Can you switch some more lights on? I don't like the dark," she said, still trying to maintain some hope that this was going to turn out all right.

The room filled with manic laughter that echoed inside her head. What was so funny about asking for light?

"No, Vida, and you're not going anywhere, so get used to it. You're going to stay here for a while. If you're good, I'll let you keep those perfect white teeth of yours for a little longer. If not, then they'll go into my collection."

Patsy burst into tears. He was frightening her and she was shaking. Surely he couldn't mean what he said. Why was he being so cruel?

"So now you know my little weakness, Vida. I enjoy playing at dentists. Perhaps you'll disobey me, and then you can play along too. I'd like that. But even my weakness for dentistry pales beside my weakness for you, Vida. You are my major failing, my true path. My nemesis."

"I'm Patsy, not Vida. Patsy Lumis! Remember me, Jack?" She was screaming and weeping. "I'm at college! I'm not Vida — whoever she is."

"Don't you dare! You stupid bitch! Vida is my life; my one true love. Do you understand, slut? So if I say you're Vida, then that's who you are — is that clear?"

Patsy Lumis nodded furiously. He was crazy; totally insane. She wanted to scream again, run, grab hold of something and hit him around the head until she knocked him out. But she couldn't. She was too weak, and she was frozen to the spot with fear.

Chapter 15

Day Six

"CCTV's in from the undertakers," Rocco told Calladine, as he entered the incident room the next morning. "We've got a blurry image of a bloke wearing dark clothing and a face mask — Mickey Mouse, I think."

"He went prepared, then." The DI shook his head. "We've possibly got another one now, so get the image enhanced — anything that helps, because we could really do with a break on this."

"Well he's tall and young, I'd say. It's the way he moves, and the weight of the girl doesn't seem to bother him."

That was something at least.

"Her laptop's full of conversations she had with him, sir," Imogen reported. "But there's nothing to pinpoint who he is or where he's from. He gives nothing away. Madison writes loads, but gets only short messages back. He must have something else, because his messaging skills are rubbish."

"Did he send her any photos?"

"I don't know. She has such a lot of stuff on here — photos she's taken and stuff from the social networking site — and I've no idea who I'm looking for."

"Order them by date if you can. That might help, given we have a rough idea of the timescale." He turned to Ruth.

"What time's the press briefing?"

"Scheduled for ten," Ruth answered.

"You look awful. What's happened?"

"I think I must've caught something from being around all those students — or eaten something bad in that canteen of theirs."

"You didn't eat though, did you?" He turned back to Imogen. "Have you cracked Patsy's laptop yet?"

"That one's not password protected, so it didn't pose any problems. But it's the same story — lots from her and virtually nothing from him. But I'll keep at it."

"Right — we'd better get down there, Ruth. Is the DCI coming?"

"Yep — if nothing else he'll want to look as if he actually knows what's going on. Have you solved the problem of the phone calls, sir?"

"I think I might have. Jo, Zoe's friend, has a contact in the States — a lieutenant in the NYPD no less. We're going to Skype when she's set it up."

"Impressive. Where's he based?"

"Queens." He shrugged. He had no idea where Queens was.

"Serena was from Queens, so this could be a break, sir."

Calladine doubted that. People in New York wouldn't have the info from the university or Serena's friends that they had. At best, all they'd have would be a missing persons report.

"How much do we tell them — the boys from the press?"

"No point in holding back, but we won't tell them about the mouth thing, not yet. This time they could be a real help. In fact we need a damn good response to whatever they print. Do you have the photos in that folder you're clutching?"

"I've got copies of the e-fit and some photos of Madison taken off her computer."

"Someone may have seen her with him, so it's worth circulating."

"Joanna Johnson has emailed us a good photo of Patsy, and one of Serena, so we'll give those out as well. We may get lucky, sir. Photos in the papers, a radio shout, and a mention in the local TV news. It all helps."

* * *

The same faces stared back at them in the room where they had met for a briefing during the *Handy Man* case. Calladine felt a pang of regret. There was no chance of Lydia being involved this time, none at all. Pity, because he missed her. And she would have been damned helpful.

He sat between Ruth and the DCI and gave an outline of the case. Most of the reporters used voice recorders, but some still scribbled away in their notebooks. Ruth distributed the photos, along with a phone number they and the public could use if they had anything to tell them.

"We're particularly interested in speaking to anyone who may have seen Patsy Lumis getting off the train on Wednesday night."

"Will there be more?" a deep male voice boomed out from the rear of the room. "Serial killers like this don't stop until they're made to. That's right, isn't it, Inspector?"

Calladine shook his head. "The truth is we don't know. I've given you where we're at currently, and I'd appreciate it if the headlines stick to the facts, ladies and gentlemen. I would like the message underlined to the students in the city, particularly the American ones, and I want people to talk to us. Do your best, please. But I don't want the local population frightened out of their wits."

"But there are things you haven't told us, aren't there, Inspector?"

He was right, of course he was. It would be foolish to release all the details. Once that happened, every weirdo in the area would be on the phone, confessing. So the mouth thing had to stay out of bounds. For the present at least.

"Irrelevant details that don't concern the public." Calladine didn't fancy the lurid headlines, and there'd be plenty of those once the truth came out.

"DCI Jones, does this have anything to do with the gangland killing earlier this week?"

Jones was taken aback and looked at Calladine, momentarily lost for words.

"No. Nothing at all. That was a quite different matter and is not the concern of this team. It would not be helpful to link the two in your paper."

The reporter who had asked this was from the Manchester press — a burly individual who worked for the daily. Poor sod must be following that case. Interesting that it had led him here this morning though. Calladine wondered if he knew that Fallon was his cousin. It was not common knowledge but it would be easy enough to find out.

The DCI stood up. He'd had enough. "A word when you've done," he muttered tersely before leaving.

What now? Was it the case, or was it the mention of the shooting that had ruffled his feathers?

After a few more questions, Calladine called a halt and whispered to Ruth, "We've given out all we need to for now. We can't waste any more time here. Let's crack on."

"What next? We've seen everyone we need to from the university. There's nothing much else to be had from the laptop for now, so it seems. So perhaps we should bother Julian and Doc Hoyle — see what forensics has uncovered for us."

Not a bad idea, except that they would have contacted him if they had anything.

"Someone here to see you, sir!" Rocco was smirking as he approached Calladine.

Sitting at the empty desk formerly inhabited by Dodgy, was Alice Bolshaw.

"I hope you don't mind, Inspector, but I contacted your DCI and he asked me to come in."

Yes, he damn well did mind. Going above his head like that wasn't on. If she wanted to work with him then she'd have to learn about teamwork.

"And?" He glowered down at the girl.

"Well . . . he said to come along. He didn't think my helping could do any harm. And he rushed through all the paperwork." She shuffled nervously in the chair.

That remained to be seen. Had the man no sense?

"Excuse me, Alice. Wait here. I'll be back in a minute."

* * *

"I don't like these continual references to your cousin, Tom. It leaves a bad taste and causes too much curiosity." The DCI stood looking out of the window, a glass of water in his hand.

"My view exactly, sir. But I don't see what I can do about it. The girl — Alice Bolshaw — did you give her permission to join us?"

"You see, the problem is Fallon is giving Central the run around and they're not happy. Now — because of your entanglement with him they're starting to lay the blame at my feet."

"They're looking for a scapegoat, sir. They'll get bored and it'll pass and, as I've explained before, I'm not 'entangled' with him, as you put it. Now back to Alice—"

"Just make use of the girl for God's sake. You're always banging on about not having enough manpower, so stop causing me problems and get on with it."

He was almost shouting, and his cheeks had turned an unhealthy shade of red. DCI Jones was overwrought and not engaging his brain properly. Alice Bolshaw was barely out of her teens, for God's sake. What use did he imagine she'd be?

Jones reached for a bottle of pills and emptied two into his palm.

"Got me on bloody tranquilizers, this damn job has. Look at me! Just look at me, man. I'm a mess."

He wasn't joking. He did look a mess, but then whose fault was that? Jones was a fool. He'd been foolish to take the job in the first place; he was well out of his depth. And it was beginning to tell.

"Alice Bolshaw was close to one of the murdered girls, sir. It's not right for her to join the team. She'll be privy to every detail, and I don't think that can be helpful in any way at all."

"I don't give a toss what you think, DI Calladine. Just do as I say. And don't answer back. Do you understand?" Jones slammed the glass down on the window sill, shaking with rage. He looked as if he was about to lose it completely, and he reached unsteadily for the edge of his desk. "Get out of here! Go on, piss off and leave me alone."

Calladine shook his head in disgust and left the office.

* * *

"Right, Alice. It seems you are with us for a while. Now, I'm going to say this once only. If I see you struggling emotionally with any of this, then I'll make you leave. Understand?"

The girl nodded her head vigorously and gave him a half smile.

"Familiarise yourself with that." He pointed to the incident board. "Imogen will give you the background stuff to look through, and then you can help her interrogate the two laptops — the one that belonged to

Madison and one that Patsy used. Perhaps you can help identify who's who among Madison's photos. You were close; you'll know who her friends were, and perhaps you'll recognise some family members."

"Details went out on the last local radio news, sir." Rocco looked up from his computer screen. "They're going to put it out on the hour for the rest of the day."

"Ruth. You and I will go have a chat with Julian — see if he's got anything from those soil samples yet. The rest of you — we need to break this — man the phones, anyone volunteers information, then get their address and ring me. Look through everything we've got so far — make sure we've not missed something."

* * *

Calladine and Ruth drove out towards Julian's lab at the hospital. "Jones is a fool. He's losing it — he's not coping with the job at all. He offers bugger all, and hardly leaves that office of his, unless it's to skulk off home early. I tell you, Ruth, if he doesn't get his finger out soon I'll go above his head."

She looked disapproving. "You wouldn't do that — it's not your style, sir."

"No, I suppose I probably wouldn't. This case is getting to me, and the last bloody straw is having to amuse Alice Bolshaw while we're up to our eyes in it. You'd think he'd have more sense. I mean, what is she? Nineteen? Twenty?"

"Yes, but you're forgetting what she's like. She's an odd sort, sir. She doesn't strike me as the sort of young woman who'll be at all bothered by what she sees or learns about the case."

"I hope you're right. I hope she doesn't turn out to be the squeamish sort."

"When are you contacting your American friend?"

"Jo will ring me, and then I'll nip home and Skype him from my laptop. I don't know what he can offer though, apart from contacting the families of the girls Alice identified."

"I wonder why he likes American women, sir. There has to be something in that — something more than there being no family close by to come looking for them."

"Perhaps we should ask Alice. After all, she does want to be a profiler."

"Seriously, sir. It is a lead — of sorts. Given that he's a nutter, then the American connection is important. It obviously means something to him."

"American women, teeth, lips, hanging onto the bodies . . . it makes no sense to me. His behaviour is so atypical."

"That's why it's important. We should look at it all again, analyse what it means. Hanging on to them, for example. That means he's had somewhere to keep them, even if it's only the back garden."

"But not anymore, it would seem, given the way Serena was dumped."

"So we should be asking ourselves what's changed. Because something has."

She had a point.

Chapter 16

"The soil sample from the body is interesting, Inspector." Julian pushed his spectacles back up his large nose. "It's very rich in phosphorus — uncommonly so."

"What's the significance of that?" Ruth asked.

"Not sure. It could be anything. But I'll investigate soil types around Leesworth and see if I can find anything similar."

"Thanks, Julian."

"Of course there could be a fairly simple explanation." He peered again through the microscope and fell silent.

Calladine looked at Ruth and sighed with irritation. The forensic scientist was at it again.

"And that is?" Calladine tapped his foot impatiently.

"Fertiliser, Inspector. You're obviously not a gardener."

"Looks like I could be right about the bodies having been kept in someone's backyard, sir."

"If it was secluded enough and the plants tended — then yes — a garden would do," Julian added.

"Perhaps he's moving, got the place up for sale, sir, and that's why he has to get rid of them."

"If he's young, like Rocco thinks, then perhaps the house is being sold from under him — by his parents."

"Or even his landlord."

Back to square one.

"Are we really going to have to trawl through all the property for sale in the area? It could take days and get us nowhere."

Calladine's mobile rang. "Rocco, what is it?"

"A woman's rung in. She says she saw Patsy Lumis get off the train at Slaithwaite Station. She's positive it was her; they'd been discussing her holiday in the USA during the journey," Rocco reported.

"What have you arranged?"

"I've got her address and she's waiting for you at home."

"We'll be back shortly. Have the folder of photos handy; she can have a good look at the ones of Patsy."

"Right, Ruth, we're off. Thanks, Julian. We'll look into what you told us."

"Before you go, Inspector — I did get a reasonable print off the ear tag. I've run it through the database but there's no match, I'm afraid. However — if you do apprehend someone — then it's another piece of evidence to fit into the jigsaw."

"The word is *when*, Julian, not *if.*"

"Could be a job for Alice," Ruth interposed, before the chat between the two men got out of hand. "She could look at the properties for sale in the area — those with gardens big enough — and then we could take a look."

"Okay — get her on it. But going round to all those properties will be time-consuming. Once we have a list, we'll keep it in case it proves useful. It'll keep Alice out of our hair for a while."

"Hang on just a moment, Inspector. I haven't told you the very best piece of news yet. I'm getting the CCTV footage from the pub enhanced. I think I might be able to give you a reasonable look at him."

Now that was a piece of good news. Just like Julian to leave it until last.

Calladine felt a surge of energy. If they could get a good enough photo distributed, they might be able to wind the whole thing up.

"You don't have to say it, Inspector; the minute I have anything I'll ring you on your mobile."

* * *

Back at the nick, Imogen and Alice were engrossed in the two laptops.

"Imogen — carry on with analysing the stuff on the laptops for now, but I've got something else for Alice." He turned to her. "Ring round the estate agents and compile a list of all the properties for sale in Leesworth which have a garden. We're only interested in gardens with plants — plenty of soil. If they've been flagged over or are covered in gravel then you can forget them."

Someone had to go to Slaithwaite. Calladine checked his watch. He couldn't afford to miss the call from Jo when it came. Devon DeAngelo worked in a different time zone and he had to be ready.

"Ruth. Rocco. Would you two go and speak to our witness and check out the area around the railway station? I'm waiting here for Jo to call, and then hopefully I can Skype the detective in New York. We'll reconvene about five. Is that okay with everyone?"

Heads nodded, and Rocco grabbed the folder.

* * *

"She was a lovely girl, so chatty," Ruby Tunnicliffe told them with a smile. "She made that boring journey into a real pleasure. We talked about all sorts, but particularly about my holiday in Miami last year. She'd been there too — stayed on a yacht, no less, and for a whole month."

"Did she say who she was meeting that night, Mrs Tunnicliffe?" Ruth asked.

"Well, she didn't say much, just that he was a new boyfriend, someone she'd met online and only seen a couple of times. I did tell her to be careful — I mean you hear such stories, don't you? Anyway, she would have none of it. Her Jack, that's what she called him, was the perfect bloke — if such a thing exists." She rolled her eyes. "But apparently he wasn't afraid to spend his money, and she seemed to like that."

"Spend his money on what? Did she say if he'd bought her anything?"

"No, but he'd taken her for some fancy meal in Chinatown earlier in the week. Eaten like a pig, she had — or so she said."

Ruth looked at Rocco — there were cameras all over that part of town.

"Did she say if they had this meal at night or during the day?" He was hoping to pin the time down and save on all that CCTV watching.

"Lunchtime. Then he took her around the shops, but I don't recall her saying they'd bought anything."

"Thanks, Mrs Tunnicliffe. Would you mind coming with us to the railway station and pointing out exactly where he was waiting? We'll bring you back home afterwards."

Ten minutes later, Ruby Tunnicliffe was describing the sequence of events.

"He was in a van, a small white van parked just beyond that street light down there. He didn't get out." She frowned. "You'd have thought he would have helped her with her stuff; her bag was heavy. We talked for a moment or two — just here on these steps, but he must have been impatient because he tooted his horn. Then she went off. She waved, and then she was gone."

"And they drove off in that direction? You didn't see them turn around?" Ruth asked. The bastard was clever. He'd have seen Patsy talking to her and wouldn't have wanted the woman to get a look at him.

"No — and I would have because I was waiting ten minutes for a taxi."

The white van again. This was their man alright. Rocco ran Mrs Tunnicliffe home, while Ruth waited outside the station and rang in.

"We're going to need the CCTV from Chinatown — say the last two days' worth. Daytime footage. And someone needs to go through it to see if they can spot Patsy. She and our man ate there lunchtime. He spent money — some posh place — and that's all we know. Also, it sounds very much like the same van. It might be an idea to check those registered to folk in Leesworth, big job or not."

* * *

Calladine got the call from Jo at about three thirty that afternoon. Apparently it was nine thirty in New York, so DeAngelo would be at work. He left the nick and went straight home to boot up his laptop. He hadn't used Skype before, but Jo had set him up an account and left instructions on how to use it. People did this all the time so it couldn't be that difficult, he reasoned. He wasn't averse to technology — it was simply that he didn't use it much. A memo, a report, a few emails, was about the scope of his expertise. Everything else he left to the others — notably Imogen.

But today technology was proving to be a little marvel. Minutes after arriving home and grabbing a mug of coffee, he was meeting Devon DeAngelo in cyberspace.

"Hi there, Detective!" The New Yorker became visible to him on the screen. "Nice to know you. Don't get to speak to our Brit cousins very often. Jo tells me she's got the hots for your daughter." He laughed at this, as if it was completely ordinary. "So what can I do for you?"

He was a large man, casually dressed in an open shirt and loose fleece jacket. He had a full head of dark hair. Calladine put him at about his own age, but he was well out of condition. He had a noticeable paunch and a reddish hue to his face. He seemed to be out of breath when he spoke.

"It's good of you to help. I really need to speak to some people stateside, but the tight sod I work for is making that very difficult."

The American laughed. Calladine could see him reaching for a can of soft drink. "We have the same problems here, believe me. The rules can be a right bitch sometimes."

"The problem I've got is that we've had a series of murders locally — all young women, all students attending a university in Manchester and all American. It's grim. They're kept somewhere, and death isn't quick. This man's a right bastard and he needs stopping as soon as possible. The problem is we've got precious little to go on. The evidence is sparse. Forensics are working on one or two leads, but nothing has given us the break we need."

"Do you know why he goes for American girls? I mean — that's pretty specific."

"No idea, but it must make some twisted sense to him. I have a list of female students, all from the US, who've left university without going through any of the formalities, and I need these checking out. I need to know if they're safe at home or missing here. We know we haven't found them all yet. We're pretty sure there'll be more before this is over."

"Jo has my email address. Send over the list and I'll do what I can, Inspector. What about those you do know about? Have the families been told?"

"We're on with that but I'll send those too. Incidentally, one of the victims was from Queens — your neck of the woods, I believe."

"Sure is. What's her name?"

"Serena Hall."

"I'll look into her background for you. Look, Inspector — suppose I get back to you tomorrow for an update?"

"Fine with me — and call me Tom."

"Great, Tom. You call me Devon."

Calladine smiled. He still couldn't quite get over the name.

"What's your rank, Devon?"

"Lieutenant. I'm in Homicide, Tom, so I do more or less the same thing you do."

"But with guns."

"You disapprove?" DeAngelo laughed, picking up a sandwich from his desk. "Better not get into that one," he chuckled. "Talk again tomorrow, Tom!" And then he was gone.

He owed Jo. He'd get her something; perhaps he'd treat her and Zoe to a slap-up meal somewhere. He was just thinking about getting back to the office when there was a series of loud raps on his front door.

Chapter 17

"You took your time, Tom Calladine. I was beginning to think you were seriously indisposed or something."

Calladine gasped, wondering if his eyes were deceiving him. But the woman who stood on his doorstep was real enough. She smiled again, batted her long lashes and pushed past him into his hallway.

"Well if you won't ask me in, Detective, then I'll just have to be a little more forward." She walked through to the sitting room, dropped the suitcase she was carrying onto the floor and stood staring at him. She cocked her lovely head to one side, winked, and then opened her arms wide. "Come here, stupid man. Come and give me a hug."

She wasn't a dream. She wasn't a hallucination brought on by stress — she was real. But it wasn't until he had her grasped tight in his arms, with his lips firmly pressed to hers, that he actually believed it.

Lydia was back.

The lovely creature he'd lost his heart to — his dream woman — was actually here. She was standing in his house with her arms wrapped around him.

"So you *are* glad to see me. From the way you looked at the door, I wondered. But whatever you think, I've missed you, Tom Calladine, missed you like crazy. No word from you, nothing, for weeks — not even a text." She slapped his arm.

"You could have rung me. It's not all one-sided, you know."

"You'd think I was chasing you! Can't have that, can we, Detective? You'll get all big-headed and start thinking you're God's gift."

"Stupid woman. You know I've only got eyes for you . . ." And he kissed her again. "It really is good to see you, Lydia. I was beginning to think you'd never come back, not after what happened to you."

"I've had to work on that, believe me, Tom. What that man did to me left mental scars — but I'm dealing with them, and not doing too bad either. The key is work, work, work then more work. I immersed myself and it's sorted my head out."

"It should never have happened." He traced his fingers down her cheek. "Another instance of Jones's penny-pinching stupidity. You should have had someone watching you."

"Let's not rake all that up now. It's in its place." She tapped her head. "It's dealt with, and that's that. I take risks; it comes with the job, so I have to live with the consequences."

"So what are you doing here? I thought you'd gone for good, and I wouldn't have blamed you."

"Like I said, I went off and licked my wounds, but now I'm back and raring to go. The job I took in Edinburgh wasn't right for me and, anyway, Scotland's too cold. I've got a new job now, so here I am."

"Are you back with the *Echo*?"

"What — that rag? No fear — that's small fry. No, Detective. I've had a sniff of the big time, and now I want more. Investigative journalism — that's where my future is. I wrote a piece for one of nationals after the *Handy Man* case and the fee was amazing. Since then I've done a few more — chased up on all the juicy cases I could find. Robberies mostly. I investigated the goings on behind that big jewellery robbery in London last month."

"So why Leesworth?"

"Because of you. I can see from the look on your face that you don't believe me, but it's true, every word. I'm not spinning you a yarn, Detective. I've really missed you, and I reached the point where I just had to come back and catch up."

"I'm flattered, Lydia, I really am. But there is an angle, isn't there? With you, there's got to be. I'm flattered, but I'm not that stupid. I mean — look at you, then take a real good look at me." He shook his head. He was feeling it again — that slightly ill at ease 'what's she up to' feeling. Investigative journalism . . . She needed him for something.

"That hurts, it really does. I like you, Tom. You know I do, and I wouldn't use you. I'm not that sort of woman."

"Lydia, you're exactly that sort of woman." He chuckled. "But right now I just don't care. It's so good to have you back, to see you standing in front of me looking wonderful, still so very lovely."

"You'll have me blushing. Let's not get into the whys and wherefores right now. Let's eat and talk and have a real good catch up."

"We'll do that later. First tell me what it is you're investigating round here."

"Can't that wait, Tom? If I tell you, then you'll just get annoyed, and bang goes our wonderful evening."

"Just tell me what you want, Lydia. I'm a busy man and I don't have time to let you run circles around me."

"Can I just say that I will need your help, Detective? I simply don't know enough about the person I'm chasing."

Why did that send a cold shiver down his spine?

"So you do want something — and you know I won't approve."

"Yes, but all I want is a few pointers; clarification on one or two things — that's all. Oh and Tom, I'd like to stay here too."

"Here? With me?"

"Well yes. You do live here, don't you?"

"Yes I do, but I'm not here alone anymore."

"You have another woman in your life — yes, I know, and I have to say I'm surprised, so soon after me . . ."

"There is another woman, but it's not what you think."

"She's very pretty, and young too. Is this her?" Lydia took out a sheaf of photos from her briefcase.

"Yes, that's me and Zoe." He blinked, not quite taking in what it was she was showing him. "Where did you get these? That's my mother's funeral. Why would you want photos of that?" He thought for a moment, and then realised. "You must have been there, watching — but why? And why not come and speak to me?"

"It didn't seem the right thing to do, Tom." She pointed to Zoe, who was holding his hand in one of the pictures. "So who's the woman then?"

"My daughter, Zoe."

"You have a daughter?" She sounded incredulous. "A grown-up daughter? Where did she come from? You certainly didn't have her last time I saw you."

"It's a long story, but she is mine — mine and Rachel's. She came looking for me when her mum died."

"Oh, I'm sorry. Are you okay with her living here?"

"Yep. It suits me just fine." He looked a little closer at the images, trying to work out why she'd taken them. Then it hit him — like a brick between the eyes.

"It's him, isn't it?" He pointed at the image of his cousin. "You're bloody well investigating him!"

The perfectly shaped eyebrows rose a little, and those baby blue eyes flashed with annoyance.

"He's big news, Detective — or he will be once you lot get your fingers out and slap the cuffs on him."

141

What on earth was she up to? Whatever it was it had to stop. She obviously had no idea what she was getting into. If Fallon got the merest whiff that Lydia was about to dish the dirt on him, he'd retaliate. She'd simply disappear. He'd have her killed and Calladine would never be able to find out how or where.

"Keep away, Lydia. Fallon is bad news. Michael Morpeth was a pussycat in comparison to my damn cousin."

"Don't be like that." She rubbed his arm. "It's all going to come out about him soon. He's started making mistakes. And with me doing the story, you can be kept out of it."

"I'm not involved." Now he was really angry. What did she think he was? "Since we reached adulthood I've had nothing to do with the bastard. And, like I keep telling people, neither should anyone else."

"So. You won't help me?" Lydia Holden stood glowering at him with her hands on her hips — those delicate, manicured hands of hers that could be so gentle, so giving.

"No, I won't help you, because I would be signing your death warrant. You'll get hurt, Lydia — you'll be picked up by one of his thugs so fast your feet won't touch. We'd never find your body. We'd never find anything."

"Then you need to up your game, Detective."

"Smart-assed comments won't get you anywhere either, Lydia."

He still couldn't believe it. Lydia Holden here, in his sitting room, calling the shots and looking so damn sexy he was helpless. He wanted her. He wanted her so badly it hurt.

"Well, if this is how you're going to be, if you're going to be all tight-lipped about Fallon, then I'll go ask elsewhere. But I have to say, you surprise me, Detective. I thought you, of all people, would be only too happy to dish the dirt on your errant kin."

"Look, Lydia, I don't have time to stand here and argue with you now—"

"Well, come to bed and argue with me there instead. Come on, Detective, I know you want to." She moved forward, and nuzzled in close. She was a siren, a weakness he couldn't resist. "Don't play hard to get, Detective. We both know it's not your style."

Their lips met long and hard. Could he take time out for this? More to the point, *should* he take time out for this woman? Her hands roamed over his chest, flipping open his shirt buttons.

"We should make up for lost time . . . Don't you want me, Tom? Want me like before — you do remember how it was, don't you, lover?"

Of course he remembered. How could he forget?

Their lips met again and this time the passion overpowered everything else in his head — the case, the problems, her need for his help. He pulled away from her. "Those pictures. Show them to me again."

Lydia groaned and reached for her folder. "'Here you go, Tom, and don't take long. This girl is hungry."

Calladine looked carefully at each one until he found it. Lydia had snapped Fallon as he stood by his car. He'd just got out and was making towards him. But it was his goon that caught his attention. The camera had caught him at the moment he lifted the arrangement of roses from the boot.

That could be it — the piece of the puzzle that would nail the bastard.

"Sorry, Lydia — I have to go out." He was fastening his shirt and grabbing his suit jacket as he moved. "Stay. Settle in. Take the back bedroom; get yourself some food. I'll be back later and we'll talk."

With that he was gone, banging the front door behind him.

Calladine pulled into the care-home car park. He took a quick look in the mirror to make sure he didn't have Lydia's lipstick all over his face, and made for the door. He had to knock. Since his mother's death he no longer had a key card.

"Is Monika here?" he asked the young woman at the reception desk.

"She's with some of the residents in the dining room. Go on through, Inspector."

Monika looked up as he entered the room. She didn't smile — but she didn't frown or tell him to get lost either.

"Sorry, Monika. I should have come before . . . Look — we could do with having a proper talk at some time. Clear the air. But for now — this is business."

She stood up from where she had been kneeling beside an elderly woman.

"I don't think we've anything much to say, do you, Tom? Actions, as they say, speak louder than words; and your actions over the past weeks have spoken volumes. You haven't been near me for weeks — you didn't even speak to me at your mother's funeral. A perfect opportunity I would have thought." She nodded towards her office. "In there, if you want to talk. Not in public, if you don't mind."

He couldn't blame her. He'd been a first-class bastard.

"It's the funeral I want to speak to you about. I know Zoe had a word. She suggested you brought some of the flowers back here. It was a filthy day — all that rain, and they'd only have been ruined if we left them on the grave."

"Yes, she did offer — and I took her up on it. I didn't touch the arrangement from you and Zoe, but I did take some of the bouquets. They are in vases around the rooms. You don't want them back, do you?"

"Oh no, nothing like that. I'm only interested in the roses — that elaborate concoction from Fallon that spelt out 'Auntie Freda'"

"Yes, I think we did take those. I can check. But before we do anything there's something I need to do. Your mother instructed me to give you this." She reached down and retrieved an envelope from a safe bolted to the floor. "She left this for you. She gave it to me the day she moved in here and said I was to only give it to you once she'd gone. She made me promise not to say anything, so I had no choice — I had to respect her wishes. She was fully aware of what she was doing when she gave it to me."

"Do you know what it is?" He gave the large brown envelope a shake. There was something inside. He could feel it moving around.

"I've no idea. She didn't say and I didn't ask. Apparently there's a letter, so that should explain it all. Now — the flowers you wanted."

This was a mystery he hadn't expected. He shook the envelope some more as he followed Monika along the corridor. Whatever it contained wasn't very big.

"We'll walk around and check all the vases."

"You haven't thrown any away?"

"I really couldn't say, Tom. I had no idea I was supposed to hang on to them. What's this all about?"

"Evidence, Monika. Evidence. Enough to nail that bastard cousin of mine with any luck."

"We must have put them in the conservatory. You're in luck — here are your roses. Shall I wrap them?" She was being facetious and it didn't suit her.

"No. In fact, don't touch them. Don't let anyone in here until I've checked these out."

The roses had large heads and were the purest white. Having been indoors for several days in a warm environment, the flowers had opened up. Calladine snapped on a pair of gloves, bent down and moved one or two of the heads with the end of a pen. Bingo! On the underside of several of them were what looked like blood stains. It looked as if the roses had picked up a very fine spray and their delicate petals had drunk it in. With a bit of

145

luck, that fine spray of blood would turn out to be from the witness, as he was thrown in the boot of Fallon's car and shot. Calladine could only hope so.

"I'm going to get our SOCO team down here. Don't let anyone in this room, Monika, and don't touch these. If I'm right, then I've got him — at long last."

But who to tell? Should he ring Central? It was their case after all. If he did that, then it would be their SOCO team he should call. He tapped in Jones's number.

"Sir, that trouble with Fallon earlier in the week. I've got some evidence that could put the dead witness in the boot of Fallon's car."

There was silence.

"Sir? Did you hear that? I need forensics down here as soon as, and I can't decide how to call it — us or Central."

He heard Jones clear his throat. "Us, Tom. Keep this with us for now. Call Batho, get him started, and then come in and report to me."

Not Central, then. Was that a mistake?

He turned to Monika. "There'll be a team down here very soon. They'll take the flowers; that's all, and they won't disturb the residents."

"So when do we talk, Tom? When do we decide what to do about this disaster of a relationship of ours? Or is it a matter of rounding things off as neatly as we can before calling it a day?"

She was looking at him strangely. He wanted to nod and tell her she'd got it right, but she didn't look at all happy. Up until the point — just about an hour ago — when Lydia had exploded into his life again, he'd have been only too happy to fling his arms around her and try again — but not now. Lydia had her claws in deep, and whatever was going on with her was just going to have to run its course.

"There is no relationship between us anymore, Monika. There hasn't been for some time. You know that as well as I do. We should settle for friendship. I'd like that. I don't like not speaking to you and having to pussyfoot around whenever we meet."

He could tell from the look on her face that this wasn't what she'd expected to hear.

"Get out of here, Tom Calladine! You're a shambles and a disgrace. Get out of my sight and don't come back. I don't want to talk to you and I certainly don't want to be your friend."

So much for that.

Chapter 18

Calladine didn't go back to his cottage — he'd leave that little treat for later. He went to the hospital — straight to Julian's lab. He wanted a quick word before the scientist got his hands on those roses.

Julian Batho was getting his gear together as the DI knocked on his door.

"Got something else for me, Inspector. A bunch of flowers, I believe."

"There's blood on some of them. You are aware that a witness who was due to testify against Ray Fallon, was found dead at the beginning of the week?"

Julian nodded; all attention.

"I'd like you to check the blood on the roses against that of the witness."

"You expect it to match? Blood on a bunch of roses from the care home? Well, I'm intrigued. How does that happen, Inspector?"

"It's complicated." Calladine frowned. He didn't fancy having to explain how he knew Fallon — and particularly not to Julian.

"I'm not going anywhere; I've got time. I've sent a team. I'll do the analysis once they return and I'll have the results promptly. So go on — indulge me. How did this little gem present itself to you?"

"It's a combination of things. Fallon is the chief suspect, but he has a cast-iron alibi. So the clever money is on the witness being put in the boot of Fallon's car and shot there. Fallon ensures his alibi's secure, then he dumps the body on the M62."

"It'd make a nice fairy tale, Inspector. How do you make the leap from Fallon's car boot to roses turning up in the care home?"

"There are things I'm not prepared to say just yet, so back off."

"Tut tut, we are touchy, aren't we?" He looked at the DI long and hard. "You know what people will say, don't you? It's already being rumoured that Fallon is getting inside intelligence from a copper, and given you know so much about all this, the finger will point at you."

"It can point long and hard — I don't care. I wouldn't give that bastard the time of day, never mind information. So don't go spreading rumours you can't back up, Julian. I know what I know because of a link I'm not prepared to disclose, but it has nothing to do with being in Fallon's pocket."

"But you do know him. You went to see him in hospital during the *Handy Man* case."

"How do you know that?" Calladine had told no one but the DCI and Ruth about that particular little visit.

"I know because I have contacts of my own, Inspector." Julian Batho thought for a moment. "Roses — then the care home — so what's the link? Come on, Calladine, I'm the soul of discretion."

"Piss off, Julian. Curiosity like that can get you into serious trouble. You'd do better to get me those damn photos from the pub instead of trying to wind me up."

Calladine left, slamming the door behind him. Julian Batho was no fool — he'd make the leap soon enough.

He'd realise that the link he was looking for was Freda Calladine's funeral.

* * *

He'd said they should reconvene back at the nick at five, but he was late. No matter, the team were still hard at it. Calladine went to his office, dumped his overcoat and went back into the incident room where he looked at the board, his hands in his trouser pockets.

"We could do with a quick appraisal — see what we've got." He clapped his hands.

Imogen looked up from the laptop she was working on. Alice was sitting quietly by her side.

"When do you all stop?" Alice whispered to Imogen.

"When the job's done. Why? You're not bored with us already, are you?"

"No, it's not that. It's just, you're all so dedicated. What about a private life?"

"Don't get me started. Most folk in here have to put all that to one side while we investigate a case. Both Ruth and Calladine haven't done very well with relationships. It's what the job does, I'm afraid."

"It's good to be part of something so important, though, isn't it? It's the sort of thing I need. I'm not good with people as a rule, but I think I could do this."

Calladine went to incident board and looked at the array of photos. The e-fit was the best bet they had so far. Someone had to come forward — someone who knew this bastard.

"We know our man finds his victims on the net," he began. "We know he goes for a particular type — he likes them to look a certain way. He likes them foreign — American, with no real network of friends and away from their family. They don't know the system, or who to turn to for advice. So he chooses carefully and sets about befriending them. If we want to move this forward, we have to ask a number of questions. First of all, why does he call them all Vida? What is it about that name? Then, why do they have to be American? As Ruth pointed out to me earlier today, it's obviously important to him in some way. Then there's the thing with the mouth."

"Trophies, sir," Rocco suggested. "It's a common enough trait with serial killers."

"That's right," Alice interrupted. "And the kind of trophy taken can sometimes be meaningful in itself."

"What can possibly be meaningful about a few teeth?" Rocco shook his head.

"This is a man who has possibly suffered some indignity at the hands of an American woman — perhaps one called Vida. Whatever happened in the past has festered in his mind, and now it's payback time. He's working through his fantasy of getting even with the woman — whoever she was."

"You've been working on a profile of this man?" Calladine asked.

"I thought it might help. I've developed it using the questions you all keep asking about his behaviour."

"Good work. Let me have a copy to look at."

Calladine already knew how thorough Alice was and how she liked detail. So perhaps she could come up with something they might be able to use. It was certainly worth looking at — they had nothing to lose.

"Ruth — what do you want to add?"

"Given that Serena had been buried in soil, he must have a place, a garden perhaps. It looks like that situation may be under threat — why else would he dump her like that? We're already looking at property in the area that's recently hit the market. It's a long shot but you never know. If his burial place is threatened, then he may want to be rid of Patsy sooner rather than later. I've also looked at the phone records of Madison and Patsy. All the calls to and from both girls were made to different pay-as-you-go mobiles — one for each girl. So there's nothing."

"Sir! I've found something," Imogen called out. She stood up and addressed the team.

"I can see from her browsing history that Patsy Lumis made regular online requests for repeat prescriptions from a local GP surgery. The medication is Sodium Valproate."

"That's used to treat epilepsy," Rocco told them. "I know because I have a friend who takes it."

"She never said anything," Alice added. "But she was absent from lectures a lot, and no one seemed to mind. I thought that was odd at the time. Now I know why."

Just what they needed. Calladine sighed. Would the bastard who'd taken her realise how important her medication was and would he let her take it?

"Get on to the GP. Find out what sort of epilepsy she has and what happens if she doesn't take her tablets. We could do with a timescale from him too." Imogen immediately picked up the office phone.

"She has her stuff, sir," Ruth reminded him. "Ruby Tunnicliffe remembered that she had a small suitcase with her. Surely she would have packed her pills."

"No doubt. But that doesn't mean he'll let her take them, does it?"

"Sir! Patsy has what are called Tonic Clonic seizures. She's been hospitalised several times since starting at the university. Each time she was admitted, and each time she's needed drugs to stop the fit — in addition to her regular medication. It doesn't look good. If she fits and doesn't recover within a certain time, the danger is that her heart will stop, or she might not be able to breathe properly."

"We're running out of time so we need to find her fast, if he hasn't killed her already himself. Rocco, get this new information to the radio station and inform the local rag. If this gets out, and she's alive, then Patsy just might get her pills. We can only try. The rest of you — Alice is looking at property for sale in the Leesworth area — give her a hand and start to check them out. You can discount any without a garden. The soil found with Serena was tended — fertilised — so someone who likes plants and cares for them. It might be an idea to check the allotments. Rocco, I'll leave that one with you to organise."

"We've catalogued Madison's photos, sir," Imogen told him. "We can account for them all in terms of who they are. I don't think she had one of him."

"Careful bastard, isn't he?"

Chapter 19

"I don't feel right! Jack — I need my medication."

Where was he? She'd been alone for hours now, or so she thought. She had no real way of knowing. She'd been sleeping again and had woken up feeling weird. She wasn't sure she could remember things correctly; she had a headache and felt dizzy. It could be the drugs he'd given her, but Patsy had felt like this before and knew what it meant. She also had a sore place on the inside of her cheek where she'd bitten it, so she must have had a small fit whilst she'd slept. If she didn't take her medication soon, then she'd go on to have a major seizure.

She crept around the perimeter of the dark room, carefully feeling her way. He'd dressed her; she was wearing a loose top and jogging bottoms, but they weren't her own.

"Jack! I need to speak to you."

"I'm busy, Vida." He stood in a doorway high above her, surrounded by a pool of light. He looked to be at the top of a staircase. "I must get on with this. I don't have time to fool around."

"I need my tablets! I have to take medication regularly or I'll get sick."

"Your imagination, Vida. There's nothing wrong with you. You're as fit as a fiddle — look at all the exercise you get at the gym."

Patsy started to cry. "I'm not Vida and I do need my tablets. I get seizures, Jack."

He moved a little closer, halfway down the staircase and pointed a finger at her. "Shut it, bitch — or I'll make sure you never say another word."

He was covered in mud. His boots were caked in it and his hands were filthy. What was he doing out there? Patsy shivered and wrapped her arms around her body. He wasn't going to listen. She'd made the worst mistake of her life in trusting him: this man was evil.

He bent down and dragged something inside. A shape — an old rug, she thought, as he bumped it down the stairs. Whatever it was must be heavy because he was out of breath. He stood for a moment, wiped his palms down the sides of his jacket and left her alone again.

He was up to something — digging. Patsy crept closer to the bundle he'd left behind. She took one of the tiny candles and held it up so that she could see. It was wrapped in an old blanket, not a rug. She took hold of one end and shook it. It didn't move. She put the candle down and, taking the ends of the fabric in both hands, pulled vigorously. The thing rolled forward making her jump away in fright. It smelled to high heaven. She bent down and moved the fabric a little more. There was something inside — something hideous, she could sense it. The hairs on the back of her neck were prickling. Another tug and her eyes widened.

The blanket was full of bones, old bones with ragged bits of putrefying flesh still attached to them. And if that wasn't terrifying enough, there was the skull. For a moment it caught the flicker of the candlelight and seemed to leer at her, taunting. She couldn't help but look a little closer. The thing had no teeth. The instruments in the cupboard! She began to feel very sick.

Patsy felt the room swirl around her. She had to keep her nerve. She knew with absolute certainty now that she would become that thing lying on the floor if she didn't do something. She had to get out of here. She had to seize any opportunity that presented itself.

It did just that a lot sooner than she expected. It had only been minutes since she'd found the bones, when the silence was broken by the sound of voices outside. Patsy closed her eyes to listen. Someone else was up there arguing with Jack. She saw faint moonlight filtering through the door at the top of the staircase. So he must have left it ajar — and it must lead outside. She heard the voices again, swearing, and then a high-pitched wail. Jack was fighting with someone. This was her chance.

It was a risk. If Jack caught her, he'd kill her, she knew that. But what did she have to lose? Patsy crept up the stone steps, eased the door just wide enough and darted through it. She felt the cold night air envelop her body and she ran as fast as her legs would allow. She'd no idea where she was or where she was going, and each time the moon was obliterated by clouds, she was thrust into pitch blackness.

She ran blindly in what she thought was a straight line. She couldn't hear anything behind her. She was soon gasping for breath and stopped for a moment, bending over with her hands on her knees. She still felt weird — she'd not had her medication and she had a pounding headache. But she daren't stop. Wherever she was, Jack would know the lie of the land better than she, so he could be on her within seconds.

Patsy ran on. She had no awareness of time passing, just the rush of wind through her hair and the ache in her legs. Suddenly she came to an abrupt and painful halt as she crashed headlong into a hedge.

She hit her leg on a tree stump and ripped the jogging bottoms on thorns. She fumbled about wildly, trying to free herself, frantically trying to untangle her hair from the grip of the bushes. Then she fell like a stone onto her front, winded. She closed her eyes and took a moment to recover. This was no good. If Jack's place was in an enclosed area, then she wouldn't be able to get out. Perhaps that's why he'd not bothered to chase after her.

She scrambled to her knees and felt along the ground — it was just grass. Patsy crawled on her hands and knees, disappearing into the dense hedgerow. The twigs and branches of the hedge dug into her body and scratched her face but she didn't care, she had to keep going. She tore at the undergrowth cutting and scraping her hands, until finally her palms hit tarmac. She was out. She'd stumbled upon a gap in the hedge and had made it onto the roadside.

Patsy lay still listening to her heart race. She felt dizzy and sick and there was a smell — the one she knew only too well, the one that always heralded a seizure. She turned onto her side and closed her eyes. Within seconds she lost consciousness.

* * *

Calladine was late home again. When he entered the house, both Zoe and Jo were back, sitting chatting with Lydia.

"You're a dark horse! Zoe called out as he walked into the sitting room. "Why didn't you say you were expecting a guest?" She winked.

"Because I wasn't." He rested the envelope Monika had given him on top of his writing bureau. "You came as a huge surprise — didn't you, Lydia?"

She smiled up at him. "You should have known I wouldn't stay away for ever. I mean, how could I?"

Calladine knew very well that she could have stayed away quite easily. But she wanted something from him. Information about his renegade cousin.

"We'll talk about that later. But before you get too comfortable, I should tell you that I won't help you with you know who. So if that's what you want from me, then you're barking up the wrong tree. My advice is to leave him well alone. He's about to get a nasty surprise anytime now, and I don't want you involved."

Lydia stuck her pretty nose in the air. "I'm going up to have a shower. When I'm done we'll talk, Detective." She frowned at him and stalked upstairs.

"I don't get it." Zoe shook her head. "What are you doing? This gorgeous woman turns up on your doorstep and you go all difficult and uncooperative. You don't know when you've got it made."

"And you don't know what she's like."

"I know you're making her feel uncomfortable, and that's not fair. She's only here visiting friends before she starts her new job."

"If she says so." He glared at her. He knew better than to take on Zoe in this mood. Soon she'd have Jo at him and then Lydia would have all the back-up she needed.

How had this happened anyway? A few months ago he'd been a loner — the place was his own, his refuge from the stress of work. Now all that had changed, and his tiny little cottage was full of women, each one with an axe to grind. Zoe had no idea what Lydia was like. She might very well be the most gorgeous woman in creation, but she took some keeping in check — and where her livelihood was concerned, she had a complete disregard for her own safety

"Devon rang earlier. He wants to speak to you again," Jo told him, coming into the sitting room to join them. That meant he probably had something — hopefully something he could use.

"Okay. I'll take the laptop into the kitchen, Skype him and see what he's got — then perhaps we can eat." Calladine was glad of the chance to disappear for a while.

"We'll have to send out for something," Zoe called after him. "We've not had time to sort anything food-wise."

"Make it Chinese, then." One day they'd have to sort out a proper shopping and cooking rota. All these takeaway meals, convenient as they were, weren't doing him any good.

"Tom! Nice to touch base again."

Devon DeAngelo looked a little smarter than the last time they'd spoken. He was wearing a grey suit and a shirt and tie.

"Have I got you at a bad time? Are you going out?"

"I'm off to court. Homicide case we worked on. I'll be glad to get the whole thing out of the way; the damn case was driving me insane — but you know that feeling, I bet. Now it just has to go right in court and I'll cross my fingers that we get the result we want. The shit will hit the fan if the bastard walks."

Shades of Fallon there. Calladine understood that feeling very well.

"Anyway, I've had your list checked and we can account for all the names, bar six."

"Six! I don't think we're looking for that many — well, I hope we're not."

"I've emailed them over, plus the DNA profiles for four of them. If you find any more bodies you'll have something to check against. Let me know what you find, then, if necessary, I'll contact the families and break the bad news."

"You've been a great help, Devon. There's no way we could have come up with that information so quick. I'll do my best and get back to you as soon as. Best of luck in court. Hope it works in your favour."

Calladine closed the Skype window and accessed his email and looked down the list. There were six names — all on Alice's original list, and all of them missing from home back in the States. As well as the DNA profiles,

Devon had made notes beside each name — a brief sketch of their home lives, not good in the main. He wasn't surprised some of them hadn't gone back.

"Chinese it is then. Want your usual?" Zoe shouted through. "I think me and Jo will go over to hers for the night — give you and Lydia some space. A little quiet time to sort out your differences."

"There's no need. You can both stay; we don't mind."

"You speak for yourself, Tom Calladine." Lydia stood in the kitchen doorway. She'd showered and was wearing a skimpy robe. "I have a night of wine and debauchery planned for us both, so perhaps it would be better if your daughter was elsewhere."

Zoe and Jo laughed at that. Why fight it? "See you tomorrow, then!" he called out as they left.

He sent the list to his printer. "I have a little work to do, and by the time I'm finished, the food should have arrived and we can eat. After that — we'll see where the night takes us."

"You know very well where the night will take us, so don't be coy. You do what you have to while I fix my hair. Keep the food warm when it arrives."

He'd given Lydia the back bedroom, but she had no intention of using it. After she'd blow-dried her hair, they shared the food and took a bottle of red wine and two glasses up to Calladine's bedroom.

"I like your house — it's cosy."

"You mean it's small."

"No, I said cosy. Sort of warm and comforting." She ran her fingertips down his naked chest. "This bed is cosy too, and I like the way you've done the room."

"It wasn't me. My mother did most of the decorating in the house, ages ago."

"Well, I guess it does all look a little dated . . ."

"Dated!"

"Yes, Tom, dated. Very eighties — or is it even seventies? I mean, just look at the wallpaper and all this furniture. Dark wood, sturdy and very ancient."

"It suits me. Moments ago you said you liked it. You've become a very hard woman to please, Lydia Holden. Time away has done you no good at all."

"I never saw your place the last time, did I? A girl doesn't like to be rude, but perhaps you could do with a makeover? I could help."

"Perhaps — but not yet. We've both got too much on."

"Case giving you trouble?"

"Yep, and a number of other things too. You for instance." He turned so that he was looking at her full in the face. "I want you to leave the Fallon thing alone. It's good advice, and for your own safety you should heed it."

"That is the problem, Tom. I find that people are always giving me advice, mostly what suits them. So I don't take too much notice. I'm too single-minded, I thought you realised that."

"Leave Fallon alone, Lydia. He's a ruthless bastard and he's going to get what he deserves very soon. I don't want you being any part of it."

"So you do know something! Go on, tell me. I won't write anything — well not yet — but one way or another I intend to find out what I need."

"Not from me you won't. This is no joke, Lydia. Fallon's a killer. Get in his way and he'll think nothing of getting rid of you."

"It's no use going on at me, Tom. We're going around in circles. It's just so much white noise in my head. All I'm working on is a human interest story, nothing heavy."

"Nothing to do with Ray Fallon can possibly be described as 'human interest.'"

"You're not listening, are you? I need this. I need something big to kick start this new career of mine. After the *Handy Man* case and what I earned out of the story, I had a sort of epiphany — I realised where the big money is. And more than that, I discovered that I've a real talent, Tom. I also have a shrewd idea how much the editors of the bigger papers will pay for an exclusive on Fallon."

He wasn't going to win this one. He could only hope that the forensic boys would get the evidence they needed to drag Fallon in and lock him up before Lydia did something stupid.

"Isn't all this just wasting time, Detective? I'm lying here, naked in your bed, and all you can do is talk work. Not very flattering, Tom Calladine. I want you to make love to me, not talk me to sleep."

No answer to that. He flicked the switch on the bedside lamp and took her in his arms.

Chapter 20

Day Seven

Calladine left Lydia sleeping. He'd phone her from work and arrange something for later. Spending the night with her had done him the world of good. He was revitalised — the blood was coursing around his veins and he was raring to go. He made himself a couple of sandwiches for lunch and grabbed the envelope from his mother — a quick goodbye to Lydia, and he was gone.

Imogen called to him as he came in, "We've had an odd one this morning, sir. Jane Rigby rang — she has our office number from when Cassie was missing. She says her husband didn't go home last night. What do you make of that?"

Calladine recalled the rather odd couple, and the way they behaved towards each other. Perhaps not getting Cassie back had been the final straw, and he'd left her.

"File the paperwork and pass it on to uniform. They can keep their eyes peeled. Circulate details of his car."

He nodded to Ruth to follow him into his office.

"I've got the information from Devon. Six of them haven't returned to their homes in the States, so we need to do some digging. Is Alice here yet?"

"She's gone out somewhere with Rocco. They've been visiting the local estate agents."

"When she returns get her to look at this." He passed her the list.

"And you? What are your plans?"

"I need to lean on Julian for more information — the soil sample and the CCTV from the pub, for starters."

He put his mother's envelope on his desk.

"Something I should know about?"

"Nothing to do with the case — it's personal."

Ruth scrutinised the list of names. "There are six names here. I thought we were looking for three, sir." She shuddered. "Aren't you going to open that?"

"I'm trying to pluck up the courage. I keep putting it off; it's something of a mystery. It's from my mother, a letter from beyond the grave. She didn't want me to have this until after she . . . well, until she was gone. So she left it with Monika. I went round last night and she gave it to me."

"That's good — you went to talk, so I presume things are better. I'm glad you took my advice. Did you get anywhere? Are you and Monika back on track? Is that why you look tons better today?"

She wasn't going to like this. No doubt she'd think he was a right idiot.

"Er, no — not really . . . Well, no not at all. Me and Monika are definitely over for good, I'm afraid." His face was a picture of guilt.

"I don't understand. What went wrong? Why didn't you make her listen? You obviously didn't do the right sort of grovelling."

"No, that's not it. I changed my mind about the whole thing. I actually went to the care home for an entirely different reason."

"So what happened? And don't spin me a tale either, Tom, because I know you."

What was the use? She was going to find out sooner or later.

"Lydia's back. She turned up on my doorstep yesterday, and — I just can't resist her."

"The blonde bimbo? Tom! Where's your self-control?"

"Where she's concerned, in my boots."

"So, why's she back now? What does she want?"

"I'd like to say because she can't live without me — but that's not it. She's chasing my bloody cousin. He's going to be the subject of some scoop she's planning to write. Investigative journalism, she calls it, and I'm a soft target for the information she needs, apparently."

"So she bats her lashes and you go to mush — is that about right?"

Calladine nodded. "I'm not proud of it, but I'm a push-over where that woman is concerned. She's a weakness I can't control. Monika paled to insignificance the instant I saw Lydia."

"You're a disgrace! Lydia Holden's bad news. Your future is with Monika and you know it. You're not stupid. That blonde will dump you the minute she gets what she wants. You won't know what hit you, it'll happen so fast. Remember last time? She didn't hang around then, did she?"

"I know all that, but having it stuffed down my throat doesn't help. I like Lydia — really like her, so get off my back."

Ruth knew she'd have to rein it in. "Okay, but don't say you weren't warned, when it all comes crashing down around your ears — and it will. Anyway, you should open the envelope. That letter must contain something very important. Your mother left you that for a good reason."

"The truth is it's scaring the hell out of me. Why would she do this? Why couldn't she simply tell me whatever it is, when she was alive?"

"I've no idea, Tom, so you should read it and then you can stop fretting."

He picked it up and looked at the delicate handwriting. His mother's hand. He'd not really felt the loss before, but now he felt it keenly. His stomach knotted and there was a lump in his throat. She was gone and there wasn't a thing he could do about it.

My dearest Tom,

If you're reading this then I'm no longer with you. I know how upset you'll be but please try to temper that with the memories you have of all the lovely times we spent together. I want you to be happy, son, and I don't want you to mourn my passing. Do things as you think fit with regards to the funeral but put me in with your dad.

Now — to the real point of this, I have a confession to make. I have agonised over this all your life, and while you were with me I never had the courage to tell you. I knew you would be upset and I knew it would change things, which is why I decided to do it this way.

With this letter there is a key — it fits the cupboard in the back of the grandfather clock I gave you — the one in your hallway. Inside the cupboard is a box and in there you will find the documents to support what I'm going to tell you now.

Fifty-two years ago your father had an affair. It didn't last long and I forgave him. I never reproached him about it and you never found out. However — the outcome of that affair was you, Tom. One night he came home with you in his arms. He also had a few baby clothes, your birth certificate and some photographs of your birth mother.

I hope you are sitting down to read this, son. I can only imagine the shock you must be feeling now. Anyway — I took you. Your dad and I never had any children of our own, so you were a gift I couldn't refuse.

Despite how you'd been brought into my life, I loved you from the very moment I set eyes on you. You look very much like your father — so how could I not? He never explained to me why your birth mother gave you up and I never asked. But he assured me that she would not come looking and she never did.

Forgive me, son, and please, try to understand why I kept this to myself. I couldn't bring myself to spoil things — the things we had as a family. Look in the box and try not to think any worse of me.

Your loving mother.

Tears blurred his vision.

Ruth looked at him tenderly. "Cup of tea, Tom." She patted his arm and rose to go and put the kettle on.

"Stick a scotch in it . . . Well she's really gone and done it this time, hasn't she?"

"Look — you don't have to tell me just because I'm here. Like you said, it's personal and I won't pry. But if I can help, if there's anything I can do, then tell me."

Calladine tossed the letter over to her. "You are one of my closest friends as well as being my work partner — so go on — read it, please. I need to share this with someone, otherwise I'll go barmy."

Ruth sat down again opposite him and read through the letter.

"It's one giant confession she's making there; one that changes everything, don't you think?" His voice was faltering. "Why didn't she just tell me, explain it while she could? Reading that, it's clear that the mistake was dads, not hers. At least then I could have got used to the idea – asked all the questions."

"Perhaps she couldn't, she'd be protecting him. She must have loved your father very much," Ruth looked up. "She'd know that it would inevitably change how you felt about both your parents and possibly everything else too."

"I'm a grown man — she could have told me. What did she imagine I was going to do? Go off the rails?"

"She brought you up — from infancy, so she is still your mother, Tom,"

167

"Not according to that, she isn't. Not by blood anyway."

They both fell silent.

"But does that really matter? Freda raised you, loved you and helped to make you the man you are. Surely that must count for something?" Ruth offered.

"Yes, of course it does, I'm not daft. But all these years and I never knew — I didn't even suspect, not once. She should have told me — they both should have told me. Everyone has a right to know the truth about their parentage."

"Well, she's told you now, hasn't she? And if you think about it, she didn't have to. So the knowledge must have been a burden for her, and it will have taken some courage to write that."

Ruth was right. There was no date on the letter, and he wondered when she had written it.

"You need time to take this in. Why don't you go home? Look in that box and get your head together."

"I can't spare the time." He reached in his desk drawer for the whiskey bottle and poured some into his tea. "Want some?"

"No. We might have to drive somewhere. Look — spending half an hour at home won't hold up the case. Go and settle this. I'll take you in my car and you can get it over with."

"Okay. As long as you stay with me while I open that damn box. I might need the voice of reason to keep me sane."

"Hold your hand, more like. Okay, we'll do this together. You can open Pandora's Box and air your skeletons — then it's straight back to the case. Alright?"

He nodded. Until he'd seen for himself what the box contained, he'd be unable to concentrate anyway.

"What I can't understand . . ." he began, as Ruth pulled up outside his home. ". . . is why my dad never said anything. And who was this other bloody woman anyway?"

"Are you sure you'll be alright doing this? If it's going to bother you we could leave it."

"See, even you're getting cold feet now! But yep — I have to do this, like you say, get it over with."

"Your dad will have had his reasons for keeping quiet, guilt probably. He'll have discussed it with your mum when you were tiny, and then as you grew up, it'll have been buried deep. That's what families do."

* * *

Calladine unlocked his front door and made straight for the clock. He took the key from his coat pocket, moved the clock away from the wall and unlocked the door at the back of the casing.

"Here we are then — the complete, hitherto unknown, history of Tom Calladine — the man who wasn't who he thought he was."

"Of course you know who you are, Tom. You're being melodramatic now. You're who you've always been — a good man, a damn good copper and a loving son."

The box was a biscuit tin that looked as if it dated back to the fifties. He carried it through to the kitchen table and prised it open. There were a couple of letters inside, a small number of photos and the all-important birth certificate.

"I was registered as Thomas Frank Calladine — Frank after my father. But they weren't married, so how come?"

"Because your dad will have gone with her to register your birth. Who was she, then? What's her name?"

He stared at the document — at a name he'd never before seen or heard of.

"Eve Walker. Mean anything?"

"Not off the top of my head."

"I don't understand how you never saw this before. You need your birth certificate for all sorts of things. What about when you needed a passport?" Ruth asked.

"Easy. My mum saw to all that. We went to Majorca when I was twelve and she got everything organised. When I left home I only ever had the cut-down version of the certificate, and that doesn't have parents' names on it."

Ruth picked up one of the photos. It showed a young man, not unlike the inspector, and a pretty blonde woman. They were on a beach somewhere. He had his trousers rolled up and she was holding her shoes in her hand. They looked happy, carefree.

"She could still be alive, you know. Have you thought of that?"

"Alive and local. Who knows, she could have watched me grow up, been someone I saw every day, and I just wouldn't have known."

"And, of course, there is something else." Ruth raised her eyebrows, giving him time to think. "Siblings. You could have brothers and sisters; something else you just don't know."

He sighed and stuffed his hands in his overcoat pockets. He didn't have time to think about all this right now. It was a big deal, and it would need some pondering. He took the photo from Ruth and studied it for a moment. What had gone on between his father and Freda in those distant days when he'd brought him home? How had he explained what had happened and what he'd done? How had she taken to him — a newborn infant? In the letter she'd said she'd loved him instantly, but she must have been angry, jealous even. One thing was certain — Freda Calladine must have loved his father very much, and because of that she'd been prepared to love Tom too.

"This whole mess does have its upside, Ruth." He broke into a sudden grin. "It means Ray Fallon is no longer my cousin."

"It means he never was — so make sure you tell the right people at work and get your career back on track."

This cheered him up no end, and he whistled his way through re-packing the tin box. "Right, Ruth!" His sergeant was now idly wondering around the house inspecting the mess Lydia had left behind.

"She's got some cheek, that bimbo. She's left make-up all over your kitchen worktops and the dishes are still clogging up the sink. Look at the clothes strewn all over the sitting room — she obviously couldn't decide what to wear today. Where's she gone anyway? Did she tell you she was going out?"

"I'm not her keeper, Ruth. Lydia can do as she pleases." He closed the tin box. "Will you look after this for me? You can see what things are like here, and I don't want to risk Zoe finding all this until I'm ready to tell her."

"Okay. I'll put it in the boot of my car, and you can put the kettle on. If you can find it."

His mobile rang.

"Sir! Good news." It was Rocco. "Patsy Lumis has been found. She's in the general, in a coma."

A coma — and that was *good* news? "Where was she found?"

"On the roadside. The one that leads up to the garden centre from the bypass."

"Have you got forensics down there?"

"Yes. Julian's lot should be crawling all over it by now."

"Okay. Ruth and I will get down there and talk to the doctors. I'll be back in later with an update." He called out to Ruth.

"No time for tea — Patsy's in the general. She's been found."

They had no idea how bad this might be. All they knew was that she was still alive. But what had she been put through?

Patsy Lumis was in intensive care and, according to the doctor, in a bad way.

"Her injuries are minor; nothing more than a few cuts and scratches. But she's had a major epileptic seizure, and what's really worrying is the length of time it may have lasted before she was found. We have no way of knowing, but what we do know is that she was both cyanosed and tachycardic when she was brought in — lack of oxygen and an erratic heartbeat. I can't say when she'll come round. I can't say whether she'll remember very much either. I'm afraid we just have to wait and see."

"Does she have any other injuries apart from the superficial ones? Her teeth, for example, are they intact?"

"Yes, everything is quite normal. It's as I said; she has suffered mild abrasions from what seems to be branches and twigs."

"What about toxicology? Has she been given anything?"

The doctor paused and studied the notes at the foot of her bed. "Nothing obvious, but some of them don't show up for a few hours — the date rape drug for example. And there is evidence of sexual activity. She's bruised, as if the experience was forced and very rough. If I had to give an opinion, then I'd say she'd been raped."

Raped, but otherwise okay. It was something — bad enough, but nonetheless, in comparison to what had happened to the others, she'd had a narrow escape.

"What was she wearing?"

"The forensic people took her clothing away. But as I recall she was wearing a tracksuit — nothing else."

"I see the name you've put on the notes is 'Vida,'" Ruth interjected, looking first at the doctor and then at Calladine. "Why is that?"

"We had no idea who she was when she arrived, and it was the name embroidered on the tracksuit top."

"We need to speak to Julian and look at that tracksuit," Calladine decided. "If anything changes, then ring me straight away." He handed the doctor one of his cards.

"We'll find Julian and then we'll go look at where she was found."

Chapter 21

"It's a standard issue — on sale at Leesdon Gym with the option to have your name, initials, or whatever embroidered on the top. And before you ask, I haven't been stepping on your toes — I was a member myself briefly, so that's how I know."

"Did it fit her properly?" Ruth asked. "I mean, it wasn't too big or too small?"

"As far as I know it was fine. It's not new though. It's been washed several times, and I'm doing tests to see whose DNA it might be harbouring."

"Good. Let me know what you get ASAP."

"Incidentally, the blood on the roses was a match, Inspector. I've passed the news on to your DCI. But I'm still curious about how you knew. I will find out, you know!" Julian Batho's head turned again to his microscope.

"What blood? What's he going on about?"

"Blood from the witness — the one my cousin murdered."

"So you've got him then? Fallon?"

"Perhaps. It would be good to get an actual forensic link between those flowers and the boot of his car though."

"A search warrant. Surely that can't be refused now, not in the light of this new evidence? There will be fibres and stuff — if there are, then Julian will find them."

"We'll see. Fallon's a slippery bastard, as well we know."

"We could go to the site where Patsy was found, then the gym. It's just around the corner from there." Ruth traced the route in the air with her finger.

"Okay, a quick look and then we'll hopefully discover who ordered the tracksuit."

"It's looking better all round, isn't it, guv?"

"Let's wait and see. Don't get ahead of yourself now, Sergeant."

But the truth was, they were getting closer. They were closing in, and the evidence was building. Once they had their suspect in custody, the DNA evidence would nail him once and for all.

* * *

The road was narrow, no more than a single track leading down to the garden centre. The hedge Patsy had scrambled through was high and deep — she'd been lucky. But where had she come from? Where had she been held?

"Let's take a closer look. I want to know what's beyond this hedge." He led the way through.

They emerged on a piece of rough land to the side of the garden centre. Patsy had come through the hedge several hundred yards from the café, through a hedge that encompassed both the garden centre and the nursery.

The place was busy again, and so was the café. "Want to speak to Sandra Dobson, sir?"

He nodded and made for a table by the window. He was thinking; his mind a storm of questions — which all brought him back to the same one — why here? As

Calladine sat and considered things, the pieces started to fit together. The soil — fertilised soil, and the need to move — this entire area was being considered for development. He'd been a fool not to have considered it before. This place might be busy now, but at night it was as quiet as the grave — there were no houses in the vicinity. He looked towards the row of conifers that separated the two businesses. The nursery was their best bet. But where did Vida fit in, and who was she?

"Hot, a drop of milk and no sugar. Just how you like it." Ruth deposited a cup in front of him. "Robert Rigby's car is outside, sir. Apparently it's been there since late yesterday afternoon."

Of course it was. Rigby was the catalyst in all this. If he was capable of buying a child, then what else might he do? He worked for the planning department, so he'd had dealings with the owners of both businesses. But where was he, and why had he left his car here? Calladine stood up. In trouble, that's where he was. Patsy escapes, and Rigby disappears — too much of a coincidence. He must have come here and stumbled on something. It could well have been Rigby that presented Patsy with an opportunity to get away. Their man must have got careless, allowing Patsy to escape.

"We need to search this entire area, Ruth — go over it with a fine-tooth comb. I think Robert Rigby is here somewhere and in grave danger — we need to find him fast."

"You think this is it? The place where he keeps them?"

Calladine nodded. Yes, he did, and he was annoyed with himself for not seeing it earlier. Anyone operating here or next door had the privacy and all the land they needed.

He got on his mobile to speak to the DCI and request more uniformed officers for the job. "I need a search warrant for the garden centre and the nursery — especially the nursery."

"It'll take a little time — don't go wading in until I ring you back. You have no real evidence, as yet, have you?"

"I have Robert Rigby's car, and he's been reported missing."

"Okay — uniform for now and I'll get the warrant."

Next he rang Julian. "That soil sample — is there anything else? Can you hazard a guess as to what might have been growing in it?"

"Further tests have revealed well-rotted horse manure, Inspector. So possibly roses. Isn't that what you spread around roses?"

Yes it was. So it looked like the nursery was a goer.

"Jones is organising a warrant, so when the uniforms turn up we'll leave them to watch the place. Then we'll go to the gym and come back." He drank the coffee in a single gulp. "By that time I'm hoping Jones can give us the all-clear."

Ruth followed in his wake.

* * *

Leesdon Gym was packed. The equipment room was full of individuals, mostly young men, sweating away the morning in physical toil. Calladine shuddered — he'd never been attracted by the keep-fit thing.

"I want to speak to the manager, please." He and Ruth flashed their warrant cards.

A young woman in a tight-fitting Lycra one-piece, her cheeks glistening with sweat, emerged from the adjoining studio. "Vanessa Pope." She wiped her face with a towel. "Aerobics this morning. What can I do for you?"

"We're from Leesworth Police, currently investigating a series of murders. We've found an item of clothing and we believe it came from here. The clothing you sell —

your clients buy the tracksuits and then have them embroidered with their names, is that right?"

"Yes. We sell a number of gym items, not just tracksuits. Members get changed, and they shower, so having their names on their garments helps, Inspector. But I can't see what our gym wear would have to do with murder?" She looked from Calladine to Ruth, but neither volunteered an explanation.

"Do you, or have you ever had, a member with the name Vida? That's all we have, we don't know her surname, I'm afraid."

"Vida?" She thought for a moment. "Oh, you must mean Vida Alton. I haven't seen her in a while, not since all that trouble. She is okay, isn't she? It isn't Vida you've found? She isn't one of your victims or anything?" Her eyes widened, and she looked genuinely concerned.

"I hope not. But the truth is we just don't know. We need to find her quickly. Do you have her full name and address?"

"Like I said — Vida Alton, and she lives across there — that white farmhouse up on the hillside." She pointed to the view of the surrounding countryside that could be seen through a large picture window. "It's the only house up there, so you can't miss it."

"Vida Alton. Any relation to James Alton?" Ruth asked.

"Well, yes, of course. She's his wife."

"You mentioned there had been some trouble. What happened?"

"Vida started receiving a number of texts — weird stuff, you know, the sort of stuff you might get from a stalker, and then there was that dreadful business with the cat. I don't know all the details — you'll have to ask her, but she became a little introverted after that and she stopped coming here. In fact I think she stopped going anywhere for a while, and who could blame her?"

So someone had targeted her — *stalker* was the word Vanessa Pope used — well that would fit. But whatever had happened she hadn't been taken like the others — so what was the connection?

"Thank you, Miss Pope. You've been a great help."

Calladine and Ruth went back to the garden-centre car park.

"Warrant or no warrant I'm going to bring James Alton in. This is all too much of a coincidence. We need to ask him a few questions. I'll get on with that. I'll take one of the uniform boys with me. You go and have a word with Vida Alton — see what she has to say about her husband and his movements, and that trouble she had."

* * *

Calladine took the path that led from the garden centre to the nursery, beckoning one of the uniformed officers to join him. Once again the gate was unlocked, and Calladine spotted the white van parked on the tarmac by the main entrance. As they walked he rang the office and spoke to Imogen.

"I know you checked Alton out and everything was okay, but we were looking at something else then — the Cassie Rigby case. Can you find out for me exactly where he was on the morning of the pile-up on the bypass."

Today there were at least three people working on the land, and one of them was James Alton. As he saw them approach he threw his spade to the ground in annoyance and made towards them.

"Whatever it is, I'm busy." He brushed his dirty palms down the sides of his overalls. "I can't help with the child so you're wasting your time."

"You are Mr James Alton?" Calladine asked, showing the man his warrant card.

"What of it? What do you want now? You've no right coming in here, wasting my time."

"I'd like a quick look at your van for a start, sir."

The man shrugged and led them across.

"It's a workhorse, this van. I transport plants around in it, so I don't know what you expect to find."

He swung open the back doors and then the passenger door. Calladine looked in the back. It smelled, and not of roses.

"It smells a bit off to me." The unmistakable pungent aroma of death hit him in the face.

"I don't know what that is. It's been like that since the other morning."

"Don't let anyone near this vehicle," Calladine told the constable.

"Mr Alton, I'd like you to come down to the station and answer a few questions."

"Like I've already told you, I'm too busy."

"It's in your interests to come voluntarily, but if you won't then I'll have no option but to arrest you."

"This is harassment. What is it I'm supposed to have done?"

"We're investigating the murder of a number of young women, Mr Alton."

The man's face went ashen. Guilt or shock, Calladine couldn't tell.

"Look — a motoring offence I could understand, but this . . . there's no way I'm involved in murder; no way." At a nod from Calladine the young constable led James Alton to the police car parked back at the garden centre. Once they were out of earshot he rang Julian Batho.

"I've got a white van I'd like your people to look at. It's parked at the nursery beside the garden centre. It smells of death to me. Also — would you take some soil samples and see if they match the one you got from Serena's body?"

Calladine left a couple of uniformed officers at the garden centre while he took Alton in for questioning.

"Keep an eye out. Watch the nursery staff and, until you hear from me, don't let anyone leave. The search party should arrive soon."

* * *

The Altons lived in some style in a modernised farmhouse on a hill above the nursery. The gardens were large and well-tended and there was a new Mercedes sports car sitting in the drive. The plant business must pay well, thought Ruth, as she parked near the gates and walked up to the front door.

She rang the bell and waited. She could hear music, and the sound of people talking and laughing. Finally a woman answered.

"Mrs Alton?" Ruth showed her warrant card. "Vida Alton?"

The woman nodded and Ruth smiled with relief. So Vida was real — she wasn't dead like they'd feared, or a figment of some nutter's imagination. She was a real flesh-and-blood woman. Ruth could hardly believe they'd actually found her — but what did it mean for the case?

"I'm Sergeant Ruth Bayliss from Leesworth Police. Can I have a word?"

With a look of bewilderment on her face, the woman stood aside so that Ruth could go in.

"What's this about? Is it Jimmy? Is he okay?"

"Yes, he's fine."

Vida Alton had an American accent, and she was the right physical build too. She looked similar to the others, with fine features and long fair hair. Whatever was going on, this had to be the right 'Vida.'

"Mrs Alton we've been looking for you for days now. At first we didn't understand that 'Vida' was actually a woman's name. When we did realise, we then had to consider whether or not some sort of harm had befallen you."

Vida Alton shook her head, confused.

"Look — is everything okay?" I believe someone's been bothering you lately? You received some strange text messages and they upset you. Did you keep them by any chance?'

"No, it was nothing, honestly — just someone playing a joke. Well that's what Jimmy said, so I deleted them all."

"There were a few then — when did they start?"

"Just under a year ago — early last spring." She led the way into the kitchen, where she was entertaining some friends. It was a huge room, beautifully fitted out and full of high-end equipment. Three women were sitting around a table, drinking coffee. They nodded at Ruth.

"Want some?"

"No, thanks. Was that all there was — the texts? Are you sure you can't think of anything else, anything odd that's upset you recently?"

"Why would anyone bother me? No one would dare, not with Jimmy looking out for me."

"You're from the States, aren't you? Can I ask how you and your husband met?"

"I went into the nursery one day to buy some plants — simple as that. I liked the place — I liked Jimmy at once, and I thought he had a good thing going, so I invested. That was several years ago now. And yes — before you ask we're very happily married. What's this all about? Is Jimmy in some sort of trouble?"

"We're not sure yet. I can't really tell you very much, I'm afraid. But I will tell you this: a number of young women have been murdered locally, and each of the bodies we've found so far, had your name written on an item they were wearing. Another young woman was found collapsed this morning near the garden centre and she was wearing a tracksuit with the name 'Vida' embroidered on the top."

"I lost one of my suits about a year ago," exclaimed the woman in surprise. "I left my sports bag in the car on the drive while I brought in the groceries, and when I went out for it, the thing had gone."

"Was there anything else in the bag?"

"No. I'd been working out at the gym, so just the suit."

"And you're sure that you have no other concerns? We can talk privately." Ruth was aware of the curious stares of the other women.

"I promise you, I'm fine. Go spend your time looking out for those who need you. I've got Jimmy."

"Tell her about the cat, Vida," one of the women called out.

"That was nothing. Well not nothing, but nothing sinister I'm sure."

"Well I think you're totally wrong there, Vida. I told you at the time to tell the police, didn't I? I mean it was weird what happened, and not natural."

The woman looked at Ruth, clearly wanting to get something off her chest. "Someone killed her cat. But they didn't just kill it, they left it mutilated and in agony on her doorstep. What sort of creep does that?"

"What do you mean by mutilated?"

"The thing had no teeth and its mouth had been sewn up. Now in my book that means someone has a problem."

First the cat and then the girls. It looked like Vida had had a narrow escape. If James Alton was their man, then she was safe. But if he wasn't? Ruth decided she needed to have this woman watched.

"Has there been anything else?"

Vida shook her head vigorously. The memory of the cat had made her cry. "It'll have been kids," she sobbed. "I don't like to talk about it. The whole thing is too horrible to think about."

"Okay, Mrs Alton. I've finished for now, but I'm going to leave a police constable here as a precaution. I'll give you my card and we'll probably need to speak to you again."

Ruth went back to her car and called in. She told Imogen about Vida, and left instructions for a uniformed officer to watch her house. They were finally closing in, but was Alton really their man? Calladine seemed to think so, but she wasn't so sure.

Chapter 22

James Alton had asked to have his solicitor present when he was interviewed and he'd been put into a room to wait. He'd refused to give a DNA sample, so Calladine was hoping that Julian would turn up something on the van pretty quick.

"Sir!" Imogen called. "The van is covered in prints. Two sets dominate; most likely Alton and one of his employees, but there are more, so Julian is checking whether any of them is a match for Patsy."

"I want to know what he's had in the back of that van. Ask Julian to get back to me on that one asap."

"Inspector!" Alice called to him. "I know it's not my place to say, but isn't James Alton too old to fit the profile? Madison spoke of him being young. He's old enough to be her father."

Calladine stared at the young woman for a moment. She was the only one to have noticed this, and she had a point. It was something that had also bothered him. But Alton and his nursery figured in this somehow. They just had to work out how.

"Well spotted, Alice. Don't worry. I have every intention of approaching this with a side order of caution. But for now, Alton is all we have."

Whether or not Alton was their man, the Vida they'd been looking for was his wife. It was also looking highly likely that the bodies had been buried in the ground at his nursery. There was no getting away from it — the pieces were beginning to fit together.

When James Alton's solicitor arrived, Ruth accompanied Calladine into the interview room.

"Mr Alton, can you tell me what happened to your wife's cat?"

"For God's sake, don't tell me that's what this is all about! I've got a business to run. At this time of year I can't afford time off to piss around here with you lot."

"Believe me, Mr Alton, we're not pissing about. You saw the cat and what had been done to it?"

The man muttered his affirmative reply.

"Well consider this. The same thing has happened to a number of women over the past few months. Can you imagine that, sir? Can you imagine what it must be like to be held against your will and be mutilated in such a way?"

Alton's ruddy face turned grey as he looked from Calladine to Ruth. "Surely you can't think . . . Look — it wasn't me. I don't know anything about the damn cat. I never liked the thing, but I wouldn't harm it — or anything else for that matter."

"I'd like to believe that, but we have one or two problems, Mr Alton. For a start your van was used to transport at least one of the bodies. And that body had been buried in your well-tended soil." Calladine's fingers formed a steeple in front of his face. "Can you think of any explanation — because I can't — other than the obvious one?"

"Look, I've already said, this has nothing to do with me. We're happy, Vida and I. I don't know any other women. We've been happy since the day we met. She's a great woman and a loving wife."

"We are investigating several murders of young women, Mr Alton. Each one was found mutilated as I described, in the same way as your cat. Each was garrotted, and each had the name 'Vida' written on an item on their person." He paused, giving Alton time to take this in.

Alton lowered his head and let out a low wailing sound. "You've got this wrong. It has nothing to do with me or Vida. This is the work of some deranged nutter, perhaps someone with a grudge, I don't know. But it's your job to find out. You shouldn't be hassling me."

"If you would agree to be more helpful, I wouldn't have to hassle you. A simple DNA test will clear all this up."

"No. I refuse. I've already told you."

"It's very odd, don't you think? This obsession he has with her — this insane need to seek out women who we think look like your wife and also sound like her. That isn't normal, Mr Alton, is it?"

"She's in danger — is that what you're telling me?" Alton looked round at his solicitor, the anxiety evident in his face.

"I've left an officer at your house," Ruth confirmed. "I spoke to her earlier and she's fine."

"You were on the bypass the morning of the pile-up?" Calladine continued. "What were you doing there so early?"

"I was delivering to a garden centre in Huddersfield. But I didn't use the bypass. I went over there by the old road."

"Your van was seen on the bypass, Mr Alton."

"I wasn't in my van. I was delivering fruit trees, so I had to use the pick-up. The van was parked, back at the nursery."

"What is the name of the place where you delivered the trees?"

"'Blooming Marvellous' on the Halifax Road."

At that moment Imogen stuck her head around the door and beckoned to Calladine.

"Julian has found a scrap of fabric in the back of Alton's van. It's from the blanket that Serena was wrapped in."

So it was confirmed — they had the right van. But what about their suspect? "Check this out for me." He scribbled the name of the garden centre on her notepad. "I want the time Alton was there, the morning of the pile-up. When you've got it, come back and tell me."

"Mr Alton. We now have proof — which is backed up by forensic evidence — that your van was used to move one of the dead women." Calladine leaned back in the chair.

The room fell silent. Alton's eyes closed for a moment.

"It wasn't me." His words were almost whispered. "I don't understand what's going on."

Imogen put her head around the door, and Calladine went out again.

"He got there just after seven. The owner remembers the time because he complained that their café wasn't open — it doesn't open until seven thirty."

"Alexander Stone said the pile-up happened at about that time — certainly no later than seven thirty."

"So Alton's in the clear. He couldn't have put Madison in that car, could he?"

"No, he couldn't. So then, who did?"

Calladine went back into the interview room. "Mr Alton, who else has access to your van — the small white one you usually drive?"

"Well there's me and a couple of the others, that's all. But mostly it's Jonathan who does the running around."

"Jonathan?"

"Jonathan Dobson, Sandra's son. You know; the manageress at the garden centre café. Jonathan works for both of us. I can't afford to employ him full-time and neither can she."

Was this man seated in front of him entirely innocent, or was he somehow complicit in the murders? He was nervous. Something was wrong — but what? He wasn't the one who did the chasing — he was too old, and he wasn't in the van when Madison was dumped. But that didn't mean he was completely in the clear. He was obviously afraid of something. He might still have known what was going on.

"Mr Alton, why won't you give a DNA sample?"

"Because I haven't done anything."

"But a DNA sample would prove your innocence, once and for all."

"Look — leave me alone. I haven't done anything to any women. You've got nothing on me, so back off."

"I still don't understand. A DNA sample from you would clear this up in no time, and then you could go."

Alton sighed wearily. "You already have my DNA." He leaned forward, his head in his hands. He looked beaten, the brash exterior completely gone. "Look, I didn't want this to get out, but I got into a lot of trouble years ago. I was brought up on the Hobfield estate. You know what that place is like. I got busted for burglary a couple of times. I was young and stupid — fortunately I got off with community service and a fine. I've never told anyone this — not even Vida. So please, can you be discreet? I run a reputable business and people trust me. Can you imagine how folk would be if this got out? Go and check, and then you'll see. I'm not a match for whoever did that to those women."

"You should have told me this earlier. It would have saved you a lot of heartache."

So if Alton wasn't their man, then who was?

"Tell me about your workforce. Jonathan, for example. What does he do, and what's he like?"

"He's okay — a little work-shy at times, but when he's on form his work's up to scratch. But he does take time off, disappears with no explanation. It's what comes of not having proper parents. Lads need guidance, and he has no father. Sandra's far too lenient with him. She's tried, God bless her, but she doesn't know the half, and these days she doesn't even bother looking. His father was a bad un from what she says — 'sown in weakness, bred from bad stock' — that's how she describes Jonathon. One night of passion with the wrong man, followed by a lifetime of worry, that's her lot, Inspector."

"I thought she had a husband. She calls herself *Mrs.*"

"That's just so folk don't talk."

Alton was telling the truth. Ruth got Julian to check the database, and the DNA of the man they wanted wasn't his. They had nothing to charge him with, so Calladine decided to let him go.

* * *

"I need the photos from that pub near the university! Whatever condition they're in, I need them now. And I think we need to talk to Jonathan Dobson urgently, don't you?"

"Photos first?" Ruth asked.

"Do we have anything?"

"Julian's cleaned them up a bit and he's sending them through now, sir."

The three of them waited around Imogen's computer screen as she opened the email attachments. They looked a little foggy, but they could see the inside of the pub and the people who were milling around the bar.

"There, sir. That's Patsy and her friend sat on the seats at the back. The shape in the foreground must be him."

All they could see was his back. Calladine hoped the next few photos would give them more.

"He's tall and skinnier than Alton, so it's definitely not him."

"There!" Imogen shouted. "This next one shows him sitting next to Patsy."

They peered closer. The picture was grainy, but they could make him out just enough to confirm for sure that it wasn't Alton.

"I've seen him before." Imogen was squinting slightly at the image.

"Rocco! This man in the photo — we've seen him somewhere, haven't we?"

"It's the guy who was working in the garden centre café that day we were chasing up on the Cassie Rigby case. What's he doing with Patsy Lumis?"

What indeed?

"I'm betting that's Jonathan Dobson." Calladine nodded. "Right — we need to find him and bring him in. Alice! Do me a favour — ring the hospital and find out if Patsy's recovered yet. If she has, is she fit enough to talk to us?"

Ruth got her coat and grabbed her car keys. "I'll drive. Nursery, sir?"

"There and the garden centre. We need that warrant quick. I hope the search team is organised. He'll know we've spoken to Alton. He could be disposing of evidence as we speak. We need to find those bodies."

"I'll get the warrant organised, then I'll join you," Rocco added.

* * *

There was already a police presence at both businesses, but they hadn't started the search yet, so no one was taking much notice. To the uninitiated eye everything looked fairly normal.

Calladine arrived, backed up by several police cars. They swooped into the car park. Ruth took the café, while

Calladine made off down the path to the nursery, with a couple of uniformed officers.

"Mrs Dobson! Where's your son?" Ruth called out.

The woman looked up from the till and nodded towards the nursery. "He's still working. Alton had to go off somewhere, so he's getting a big order out."

Ruth caught up with the inspector and told him. Then they saw the young man hauling fruit trees onto the pick-up truck. Ruth was hurrying behind Calladine, and he gestured for her to slow down. He didn't want Jonathan spooked. From the look of him he'd be good on his toes, and he didn't want him doing a runner.

"Hi there!" He called out as casually as he could, his hands in his coat pockets and a smile on his face. "Is James Alton in?"

Jonathon Dobson put down the sapling he was shifting, and brushed his hair off his face as he shook his head. "I thought you lot had him."

He was young, in his mid-twenties, and not bad-looking. He had longish dark hair and looked very fit — like a man who worked out. He was humming to himself as he worked, and didn't seem at all bothered by the sudden appearance of the police. This worried Calladine. What was he up to? What had he done? Had he covered his tracks so soon? Surely he wouldn't have had the time — and he didn't know they were onto him yet.

Then he saw it. At the top end of the tract of land, the inspector could see a bonfire which was alight and smoking away. To the casual observer it looked as if they were simply burning old stock; twigs and branches that had been pruned. But it was the smell that gave the game away. To those who knew it, there was no disguising the smell of burning flesh. Calladine felt a shiver run down his spine. This one was a monster. So cocksure, so confident he could outwit them.

"What are you burning?" Calladine asked as casually as he could.

"Rubbish. I'm getting rid of the dross — preparing for the new stuff."

"Odd smell, don't you think?"

Dobson began to chuckle, and then covered his mouth with his hand. He leaned on the spade he'd been using. "The stuff's rotten — not what I want at all." He looked Calladine directly in the eye as he spoke — his were deep blue, cold as ice and without a flicker of warmth in them. Calladine shuddered. Time to wrap this up; time to get this bastard behind bars.

The weather was cold and wet, so the fire never really stood much chance, despite the liberal dowsing with petrol he'd given it. Calladine nodded to one of the uniforms and sent him off with a hosepipe.

"Jonathan, you've taken some tracking down. In fact you've led us quite a dance over the last few days. But finally it's all over."

Chapter 23

Lydia Holden took her time getting ready. She deliberately waited for Calladine to leave — she didn't fancy answering any awkward questions. She got out of bed, showered and made herself coffee and toast. She had a busy day ahead of her. She planned to drive into the Cheshire countryside and make her first contact with Marilyn Fallon. She was excited. This was finally it. She was on her way to getting one of the biggest stories of the decade.

She checked her handbag. The photo was in place, all the details she'd need. She was ready. Lydia had done her homework. She'd been studying Fallon and his wife for days and knew their routine almost as well as she knew her own. At eleven each morning Marilyn went out to walk her dog — and that was the key. It was obvious from everything Lydia had observed that Marilyn loved the animal, despite its being a funny-looking thing with wrinkles all over its face. A dog that Lydia had learned was a breed called a 'Shar Pei.'

Today, the unsuspecting Marilyn was going to make a new friend. It'd all happen so smoothly and appear so natural she wouldn't suspect a thing. She'd meet a like-minded soul who shared her interests, including her love of dogs, and this rare breed in particular. She'd see very different Lydia; a superficial, high-maintenance blonde with too much money and too much time on her hands, and hopefully Marilyn would recognise a kindred spirit.

Lydia was piqued that Tom Calladine was being such a pain where his cousin was concerned. She'd hoped to wangle an invitation to dinner or some similar family gathering, but Tom was dead set against having anything to do with the man. He could have made this a whole lot easier — but no, he had his principles, so she'd just have to move things on herself.

The journey was one Lydia had made several times since returning to the area. She left Leesdon via the bypass, made for the M60 ring road, then the M56 and out to Cheshire. The traffic was heavy, and road works on the M60 made the going slow. She checked her watch — she didn't want to be late. Lydia had planned this down to the last detail, and that included the exact moment when she would approach Marilyn.

At last she reached the tree-lined avenue where the Fallons lived and parked outside a huge rambling house with a 'For Sale' sign in the front garden. Then she waited. The Fallons lived directly opposite — a stroke of luck. Lydia checked her phone. Nothing, not even a text from Tom. Just as well, because there was no way she would be summoned back — not after all this effort.

A few minutes later and exactly on cue, Lydia saw Marilyn Fallon's tall figure emerge from her front door. She pretended to be rummaging through her bag while the woman organised her dog. As she locked up behind her and snapped the lead on his collar, Lydia plastered a smile on her face and pounced.

"He's beautiful!" she enthused, as she proceeded to lock her car. "I thought he was a Shar Pei when I first saw you, but I couldn't be sure. I just had to get out and have a look — I love these dogs. I have one of my own."

Marilyn Fallon was older than the impression she gave from a distance. She might be clad in skinny jeans and a sharp designer leather jacket with matching knee high boots, but close up her face revealed the true story. Her hair was scraped back and had been over-dyed. Perhaps once she'd been that lovely, long-haired blonde but now the colour was too brassy, and the texture dry and coarse. Her make-up was too bright, and looked garish in daylight. Here was a woman trying very hard and failing on all counts.

Lydia knew at once she'd been right to move in on the dog. Marilyn seemed only too pleased to have it noticed. "Yes, he is beautiful, isn't he? Not many people know the breed." She smiled.

"Like I said, I have one at home." Lydia took the photos from her bag. "This is my 'Ming.' In fact she's a blue, like yours."

"Really?" Marilyn leaned a little closer. "She's gorgeous, isn't she, Sam?" She stroked the little dog lovingly. "Do you live around here?"

"Not yet, but I'm house-hunting right now." She nodded at the run-down stone pile opposite. "In fact I'm waiting for the estate agent now. I've been looking at property round here for weeks, but I've got a good feeling about this one. I never expected to find someone else with one of these, and so close by." She laughed, and dared to stroke the thing. "It's really nice to bump into someone who likes the breed as much as I do. Perhaps it's a sign that I really have found the right house at last."

"When you move perhaps we could walk the dogs together. It'd be nice to have someone else who has an interest. Does your . . . Ming, have all the papers — you know, Kennel Club credentials and everything?"

"Oh, yes. I entered her at Crufts two years ago and she got a 'highly commended.' If I had the time we'd do more, but you know how it is."

Lydia could tell that Marilyn Fallon was impressed. She positively beamed as she stroked and patted the dog some more.

"I'd love to show Sam, but I don't know if I'd have the confidence."

"That's a shame. He'd do so well, and it's a laugh, it really is. Everyone is so friendly and helpful. There's no snobbery at all."

Lydia was beginning to believe she really did own a dog, she sounded so plausible.

But the dog was getting restless, eager to be off. "Do you plan to breed her?"

"I'd like to before she gets much older, but it's all about finding a suitable mate."

"Isn't it always?" Marilyn laughed. "And not just with dogs either."

The two women laughed.

Shades of discontent, Lydia wondered? Might be something she could use — a way in.

"Look — if you're still around when I get back why not come and have a coffee?"

This was going better than Lydia could have imagined. Marilyn was a pushover and it was all down to the dog! "That's very kind of you. It shouldn't take long to look around the place. I'll know straight away if it's suitable — you know, by the feel of the place."

The two women said their goodbyes, and Marilyn Fallon disappeared down the road. Lydia went back to her car to wait. This had gone better than she could have imagined — the woman was completely taken in. She'd hang around, have that cup of coffee and arrange to meet her again soon — perhaps a jolly little foursome for drinks one evening. And given that Tom wouldn't play the game, she'd have to find herself another presentable man for the evening. She felt sure one of her old colleagues from the *Echo* would oblige.

Lydia was pleased with her progress. This sort of stuff suited her. It was exciting, like being a spy. The intrigue, the pretending to be someone else — wheedling a story out of the unsuspecting. She loved it all.

Her pleasant reverie, and the quiet of this leafy, well-heeled idyll was shattered as several police cars wheeled into the Avenue. Within seconds the place was bedlam — sirens, police officers in body armour and helmets — even some with firearms. Lydia had no idea what was going on but, as they descended on the Fallon house, she guessed she ought to leave.

But curiosity got the better of her. She drove a few yards down the road, parked up and hunkered down in her seat to watch the proceedings unfold. The police banged on the front door. One of them gave it the sole of his boot and it flew open. They were in, and they could only be looking for Ray Fallon. But was he there? Lydia got her answer almost instantly.

"Good of you to wait." A male voice rasped in her ear.

She hadn't even heard the passenger door open, or seen the man dart across the road. Her heart gave a jolt. "I got away by the skin of my teeth. Far too close for comfort, even for me, so let's get out of here, pronto."

Lydia's heart was beating furiously. She gave the figure a quick sideways glance — yes, Ray Fallon! How had he got here? Large as life, he was sat low in the passenger seat, with a baseball cap pulled down over his eyes.

"Don't make a sound, pretty lady. Pull out nice and slow, and make for the main road through the village."

"I don't know what's going on but this won't work. They'll be after us in seconds. Anyway, I can't drive — I'm in shock. Who the hell are you?"

"Don't come the innocent with me. You know very well who I am, and more to the point, Miss Holden, I know you. You used to work for the local rag and now you're shacked up with that cousin of mine."

Lydia had no idea how he could know all that, but since he did, it seemed pointless pretending. "As it happens I was hoping to meet you today, Mr Fallon." She smiled, without turning around. She was trying her very best to sound unruffled by what had just happened, but he must have seen her body shaking, because he started to laugh.

"But this wasn't what you had in mind, I'll bet."

"I wanted to interview you." She tried to keep her voice from wobbling.

"Keep your mouth shut and drive."

In her rear-view mirror, Lydia could see the mayhem they were leaving behind, but there was nothing she could do to attract their attention.

"Okay. But drive where? Where are we going, Mr Fallon?"

"Leesdon. To see that interfering cousin of mine."

"Leesdon . . .? I don't think I know the place . . ."

"Oh yes you do, so don't give me any of that shit. Like I told you — you're living with the sneaky bastard. Grant me a little intelligence, Miss Holden. I know just about everything that goes on in Thomas's life."

As far as Lydia knew, Tom had no idea. She'd have to put him straight — once she'd extricated herself from this mess.

"Then you'll know what I do for a living?"

"You're a bloody snoop. What else is there to know?"

"Yes, but a very *tasteful* snoop, Mr Fallon. What I propose to do with your story is make you more acceptable to the millions who'll read it."

"Acceptable. The one thing I'll never be, missy, is acceptable — so don't even try. I hate the press — I'll see you dead first."

The way he spoke these words suggested he wasn't joking. Lydia felt an icy shiver of pure fear fly down her spine. Tom had been right — Fallon was a very scary man — and now he was pressing something hard into her thigh. She sneaked a look, and immediately wished she hadn't. It was a revolver. Now this thug was after Tom — and it wasn't for a family catch-up, that was for sure. So what could she do?

"I need petrol. My gauge is on the blink. There won't be enough in the tank to get us to Leesdon."

"Nice try, bitch. Do you really think I'm that naïve? And don't go anywhere near my Marilyn again. She's gullible, and I won't have you bothering her. Do you understand?"

Lydia nodded her head furiously. She understood alright and had no intention of crossing him. She checked her rear mirror again — no one was following. The police had been too concerned with getting into the Fallon house and searching it to realise he'd already scarpered. No one had seen them drive away. But surely they must have realised he wasn't in the house by now? It would all depend on what Marilyn told them when she got back. The motorway stretched out ahead. There were any number of cameras along the distance they would cover. But would they pick them up? Fallon was still low in the seat with that damn hat obliterating most of his face — so it was unlikely. Lydia racked her brain for some way to warn Tom, but her mobile was in her bag on the back seat. Her only hope, then, was to do something once they reached his house. Hopefully Tom would be out.

Chapter 24

Dobson spat onto the ground, and shrugged as Calladine snapped the handcuffs on him. He offered no explanations; he didn't plead his case or try to run. Nothing.

"Every inch of this place must be searched. Rigby must be here somewhere, and we need to find where Dobson kept the girls."

"Sir!"

It was Rocco, arriving on the scene with James Alton and, surprisingly, his wife, Vida.

"I've got the keys, Inspector. I'll unlock the greenhouses and the old outbuilding."

Calladine gestured at the uniformed officer holding Dobson to get him to a car, but he shuffled out of his grasp.

"Vida, you came! I knew you would! I knew you wouldn't let me down."

Vida Alton held onto her husband's arm and buried her face in his shoulder, as the uniformed officer grabbed Dobson's coat and held him fast.

"It's Jonathan! He's the creep who did all those things, isn't he?"

"But you know I only did it for you! You love me, you know you do. We should be together — I waited for you, I practised and everything. I did all this for you, Vida." His expression grew bewildered when he saw the hatred in her eyes. "Why didn't you come? Why did you leave me alone with those stupid slags? I tried to turn them into you, but it just didn't work. I couldn't get them perfect enough."

James Alton gave her a puzzled look. "What's he talking about? You and he, you never . . .?

"No, of course not. I hardly know him. He used to bother me at the gym — that's partly why I stopped going. He used to stare, watch me while I worked out."

Calladine told the officer to take Dobson away. "The man's delusional. He's built an entire fantasy around his obsession with your wife. When he couldn't get near her he went after a series of lookalikes — sound-alikes too. He imagined he could create a perfect copy." He shook his head. "Take your wife home, Mr Alton. I'll send an officer to take a statement later."

Calladine cast his eyes over the large tract of land spread out in front of him. "Before you go, Mr Alton, we think Dobson must have had somewhere — a safe, secure place unlikely to be found by mistake, by either you or the workforce. Have you any idea where that might be? A man's life may depend upon it."

"The greenhouses are just as you see them — built over the soil you see them standing on. The only possibility is that." He indicated the stone outbuilding. "Before I came here and developed the nursery, the land belonged to a farm, and that was one of the barns. I use it for storage, that's all."

"We'll start in there, thanks. Now you get off."

"Sir!" Rocco called. "The hospital has just been on. Patsy's come round and she's talking."

"Get round there and see what she remembers. Anything about where she was kept would be helpful."

* * *

Jonathan Dobson had finally been taken off to the police station, where he would be interviewed. As soon as his DNA had been checked against the samples they had, they'd charge him. Dobson seemed oddly unconcerned. When he'd been arrested, he'd merely smiled and made some remark about missing the football tonight. His mother, on the other hand, had been frantic. She didn't believe it —couldn't believe it — but she obviously had no idea what her son was up to most of the time. She had admitted that he was rarely at home.

Doc Hoyle arrived with Julian Batho to examine the bonfire. It was a mess, which hadn't been helped by the dousing it had received. But the doctor was able to confirm that there were human bones amongst the ash.

"Impossible to burn bones at this temperature. He must have been desperate, to try this. I'll run the usual tests and keep you informed, but there's no doubt in my mind what these are. We'll check the DNA against the profiles you got from your American friend. If I'm right, I can see the remains of at least three bodies. The flesh — what there was of it, has mostly burned away, but there is a little still clinging to that leg over there."

Calladine saw Ruth's face pale. She'd be on the verge of retching. This was another find that was far too gruesome for her. The smell was as bad as the post-mortem room, and Serena's remains.

"The outbuilding is single storey and there's nothing but tools and sacks of fertiliser stashed in there," a uniformed officer called across to them.

"It's here. It's got to be, there's nowhere else." Calladine felt the bonnet of the white van. "This hasn't moved all day, it's stone cold. He's had the bodies buried here somewhere, so he must have a place — a room, something. Rigby's car is in the café car park. I'm not wrong, I can feel it."

"It looks like the bodies were buried over here," Julian called to him. "See — the soil is freshly dug, and you can see where he's dragged something along the ground. There's remnants of burnt cloth in the ash too. Could be bodies wrapped in blankets, like Serena."

Dobson must have realised that Alton would eventually capitulate and sell his land to the council, and that's why he'd needed to move them. It bothered Calladine that, without the impending buy-out, Dobson's crimes might never have come to light.

It was only about four in the afternoon, but at this time of the year it was already getting dark. If they didn't find something soon they would need extra lights. Calladine didn't want to leave all this exposed to the elements overnight. He took his mobile from his overcoat pocket and rang Rocco.

"Have you got anything? We've searched high and low but we can't find anything. Is there something Patsy can tell us about where she was held?"

"She's still a bit groggy and deeply shocked, sir. But she did say there was no light — no windows. She only escaped because a door opened above her, if that makes any sense."

It might. Calladine went back into the outbuilding and walked around it. There were windows on two sides with no covering. If Patsy had been kept in here she'd have seen daylight and the night sky.

"Ruth! There are no other doors. It's one room — so what is it we're missing?"

"I don't know, sir. Could there be a cellar? I mean, would a barn even have a cellar?"

Unlikely, but it had given him an idea. Calladine went outside again and walked all around the building. The land fell away on the far side. Over the years, soil and stone had been piled up against the wall, but it was possible that at some time in the past it had been a two storey building with another entrance back here, an entrance to what was then the ground floor.

"Ruth — I think what we're standing in now was once the upper floor. If I'm right then there was once another way in, at the back."

"So what are we looking for, sir?"

"A way down from in here — possibly a hidden entrance. Get the others."

It didn't take long. They found a loose flagstone laid over a wooden trapdoor that led down a flight of steps.

"Get Julian in here."

"Forensics first!" Julian called out. He was suited up, and, his way lit by with several torches, he descended the steps. "Inspector! Your man, Rigby, is down here. Get an ambulance!"

Calladine nodded at Ruth, hauled a white all-in-one suit over his clothes and went down after Julian. Robert Rigby was unconscious. He had been struck by something, which had caused a wound to his head. The room they were in smelled dreadful. There was an old stained mattress on the floor and what looked a dentist's chair in the far corner. Calladine shuddered. Those poor women — what they must have endured down here with no one to help them. He was just glad it was finally all over.

* * *

"A job well done, sir." It was an hour later. "Rigby will be fine: concussion and a broken arm. He was lucky; Dobson could have killed him — would have killed him if we hadn't got him."

"That's it, then. It's all down to forensics now to piece things together. Imogen's been on. The DNA from the girls and the foetuses is a match for Dobson, so we've got him."

"I think we should call it a day. I'm whacked; what about you?"

"I certainly am. It's been a long haul — one of the worst. But we did it — we got that bastard off the streets and all the evidence we need to make a cast-iron case."

"Coming to the pub? Celebration drink?"

An excellent idea, and there was a time when Calladine wouldn't have had to think twice about it. But now he had commitments. There were people at home to see to.

"You saw my house — they'll all be back soon." He checked his watch. "So no. I'm sorry to wimp out, but it'll have to be another time, if you don't mind. I'm going to make some food, delegate the washing-up and then put my feet up."

"Doesn't a stiff drink sound better, Tom? It's been a big day altogether, what with the case, the horrors and all the personal stuff."

"You just keep the box thing to yourself for now, Ruth. I'll get it back when I've decided how to keep it away from prying eyes. And anyway — never mind me, perhaps you'd do better to go home and see Jake. Won't he wonder where you are? You don't really want to go back to him smelling of booze."

"I don't know what I want. To be honest, I'm still upset about what we've just found. I don't think I'd be much company for Jake. He doesn't like me to talk about my job, and you know what it's like. Once a case is wrapped up all the talking, the going over stuff, it's like therapy. Anyway, Rocco, Imogen and the others will expect one of us to turn up." She nudged him playfully. "Joyce will be upset if you don't come — she seems to be carrying something of a torch for you."

"First I've heard. And don't you go stirring it. Joyce is a bloody good administrator — if she gets the funnies and leaves, then we'd all miss her."

"No fear of her doing that, sir. We wouldn't let her. Is there anything yet on a replacement for Dodgy?"

"No, and I doubt there will be with Jones in penny-pinching mode."

"I see. So the team shrinks."

"The mistake we made was managing. All Jones sees is another case wound up. I've had the obligatory moan about lack of staff, but nonetheless — we still sorted it."

"We had help, sir. There was Alice and your new pal from the States."

"I must Skype Devon later — tell him the good news."

"And Alice?"

"We'll see."

* * *

Lydia drove down Leesdon High Street as slowly as she dared, mentally willing all the traffic lights to change to red. Fallon was sitting at her side, chewing gum and still pressing that damn pistol into her thigh. She was frantically trying to work out what she could do. She was tempted to pull in and make a run for it. But the streets were so well lit that all she'd be doing was making herself a damn good target.

"Step on it, second on the right up here."

"I know very well where Tom lives. What are you going to do?"

The question had been burning a hole in her brain since they left Cheshire, but she already knew the answer. This wasn't going to be good. Something had happened — hence the police raid, and Fallon knew Tom was at the bottom of it. He intended to kill him — he had nothing to lose now.

"Let's put it this way, his detecting days are over. He's crossed me once too often, and if I'm going down because of him then I'm taking him with me."

"You'll not get away with it. Things will be twice as bad for you if you hurt him. They'll come after you. You're not stupid. You should turn yourself in."

He burst into laughter, so hard that he had to wipe the tears from his eyes. "You're very entertaining as well as being a looker. I can well understand why Thomas keeps you around. There's a space outside his house — pull into it."

Lydia was a bag of nerves. Tom was in — she could see the lights were on. She felt sick — what if Zoe and her friend were home too? What would Fallon do to them? Come to think about it — what plans did he have for her?

"Look, why don't you just go now? I won't say anything, it'll be our secret. You don't have to do this, I won't tell Tom, honestly."

"Get out and get the door open."

Lydia had no choice. She scrambled out of the car and knocked feebly on the front door. Fallon followed, and stood with his back to the wall so Tom wouldn't see him.

* * *

"I thought I gave you a key." Calladine opened the door wearing an apron wrapped around his middle. "I'm doing a beef stew — that suit you?"

Fallon pushed Lydia to one side and shoved Calladine backwards into the house. Fallon was shorter than his cousin, but the detective was caught off guard and stumbled back awkwardly.

"Ray! What are doing? You bloody fool!"

"Getting my own back, and how very good it feels too, Thomas." Fallon looked around the room. "I always knew it would come to this. You never learn. You sent them after me — you stitched me up with those damn flowers, you interfering bastard. Well, this time you're not coming out on top."

Calladine watched Fallon smile. The idiot had a gun.

"Right between the eyes, Thomas. Then I'll deal with that bloody woman."

Calladine stepped backwards, his mind frantically searching for a way out. Fallon would kill him and then he'd kill anyone else in the house – Lydia!

"Say your prayers, Thomas."

He heard Lydia scream. She was standing behind his cousin. If she was going to do something then she had only seconds. Calladine was frozen to the spot. All he could see was that damn gun, raised and pointed directly at him. Then Lydia struck.

He watched her jump forward, catching Fallon's arm with her hand at the instant he pulled the trigger. It knocked him off balance and the bullet fell short of its mark, but it still hit him.

Tom Calladine heard her scream again as he crumpled like a rag doll and fell to the floor.

There was heat. Waves of searing heat, and an excruciating stinging sensation. He was falling and he couldn't hear properly. He was on his back staring up at the ceiling. The light fitting seemed to be swimming wildly in his field of vision. The last thing he saw was Lydia's face; the last thing he felt were her warm tears falling onto his cheek. But what gave him hope before the blackness took him was the sound of Ruth's voice somewhere in the distance, and the noise of police sirens tearing up his street.

THE END

Thank you for reading this book. If you enjoyed it please leave feedback on Amazon, and if there is anything we missed or you have a question about then please get in touch. The author and publishing team appreciate your feedback and time reading this book.

Our email is jasper@joffebooks.com

www.joffebooks.com

ALSO BY HELEN DURRANT

CALLADINE & BAYLISS MYSTERIES
DEAD WRONG
DEAD SILENT
DEAD LIST
DEAD LOST

DI GRECO
DARK MURDER

Printed in Great Britain
by Amazon